RoScoE RiLEY
RULES
4 BooKS in 1!

Also by Katherine Applegate

The One and Only Ivan

ROSCOE RILEY RULES

4 Books in 1!

#1: Never Glue Your Friends to Chairs

#2: Never Swipe a Bully's Bear

#3: Don't Swap Your Sweater for a Dog

#4: Never Swim in Applesauce

HARPER
An Imprint of HarperCollinsPublishers

Roscoe Riley Rules 4 Books in 1!

Roscoe Riley Rules #1: Never Glue Your Friends to Chairs
Roscoe Riley Rules #2: Never Swipe a Bully's Bear
Roscoe Riley Rules #3: Don't Swap Your Sweater for a Dog
Roscoe Riley Rules #4: Never Swim in Applesauce
Text copyright © 2008 by Katherine Applegate
Illustrations copyright © 2008 by Brian Biggs
ISBN 978-0-06-256427-6

Typography by Jennifer Heuer
16 17 18 19 20   PC/RRDH   10 9 8 7 6 5 4 3 2 1
❖
First Edition

Contents

For Julia and Jake,
with love

Contents

1

Welcome to Time-Out

Hey! Over here!

It's me. Roscoe.

Welcome to the Official Roscoe Riley Time-out Corner.

Want to hang out with me?

I have to warn you, though. We're going to be here for a while.

See, I kinda got in some trouble today. Again.

Kids have to follow so many rules!

Sometimes my brain forgets to remember them all.

It's not like I *try* to find ways to get in trouble. It's just that trouble has a way of finding me.

Truth is, I'm just a normal, everyday kid like you.

My favorite food is blue M&M's. My favorite sport is bed jumping. My favorite color is rainbow.

And my most not-favorite thing is lima beans.

See? Like I said. Just a normal, everyday kid.

A normal, everyday kid who sometimes gets into trouble.

Like today. I was just trying to help out my teacher.

How was I supposed to know you shouldn't glue people to chairs?

With Super-Mega-Gonzo Glue?

You've done that, haven't you?

Oh.

Never?

Oh.

Well, maybe you should hear the whole story. . . .

2

Something You Should Know
Before We Get Started

Here's the thing about Super-Mega-Gonzo Glue.

When the label says *permanent*, they mean permanent.

As in FOREVER AND EVER.

Something Else You Should Know
Before We Get Started

You gotta trust me on this.

Super-Mega-Gonzo Glue is for gluing THINGS.

Not PEOPLE.

It is a way bad idea to glue THINGS to PEOPLE.

That's just a for-instance.

4

This Morning at My House

You're probably wondering how I know so much about Super-Mega-Gonzo Glue.

Well, it all started this morning. I was helping my mom pack my lunch.

"Banana?" I asked her. "With no icky brown spots on it?"

Mom looked in my lunch box.

"Check," she said.

"Little fishy crackers?"

"Check."

"Gigantic chocolate cupcake with tons of gooey frosting and those little sprinkle things?"

Mom smiled her I'm-getting-tired-of-this smile.

"Sorry," she said. "We're fresh out of gigantic chocolate cupcakes."

I sighed. "It was worth a try."

Mom grabbed a comb off the kitchen counter. "Hair time, buddy. You want to look extra handsome for the open house."

In the afternoon, all the parents were coming to visit our classroom.

That's called an open house.

Even though it's at school.

We were going to sing a song about bees.

And have desserts and juice and milk.

I was especially excited about the dessert part.

My mom was bringing her banana-avocado-raisin cream pie.

I was not so excited about that.

My mom is a great mom.

But she is not a great cook.

"You have to be extra nice to Ms. Diz," I said.

Ms. Diz is my first-grade teacher. She is brand-new.

She loves teaching my class. Even though we get a little crazy sometimes.

Ms. Diz says we are very high-spirited.

"Of course we'll be nice," Mom said.

"'Cause this is her first time showing us off. And also 'cause the principal will be there."

"I promise Dad and I will behave," Mom said.

"And be sure to clap after we do our bee song," I added.

"I promise," Mom said.

"And no laughing," I added.

"Why would we laugh, sweetheart?"

"Because yesterday when we practiced it was kind of a mess," I said. "The head bobbles kept coming off."

Mom frowned and asked, "What's a head bobble?"

"You know. The ten knees on a bee head?"

I put my hands on my head and wiggled my pointer fingers to show her.

"Oh." Mom smiled. "You mean the *antennae*."

"I'm lucky. 'Cause I'm in the rhythm

section. We pound with sticks to keep the beat. And we get bobbles too."

"That's a very important job." Mom kissed the top of my head. "Don't worry. I'm sure everything will go perfectly today."

Mom zipped up my lunch box. "Okay, kiddo. You're good to go."

Just then I remembered something.

"Wait!" I cried. "There is one more really important thing! I was supposed to bring art supplies yesterday. For the art cupboard. 'Member? You said we would bring them 'cause it's easier than being a room mother?"

"Oops. I almost forgot," said Mom. She grinned. "Roscoe to the rescue!"

My family likes to say that when I help out.

My dad came in and poured a cup of coffee.

He was wearing a business suit, a brown sock, and a bare foot.

"Morning," he said. "Roscoe, is your brother up yet?"

"Yep," I said. "But I had to use my Roscoe Riley Sneak Attack to wake him. Would you like to try it sometime?"

"I'm listening," Dad said.

He made one eyebrow go up.

It's a trick a lot of dads can do.

"Well, first you knock real polite on Max's door. Then he growls and tells you to come back next year."

"And then?" asked Dad.

"Then you jump on his bed like it's a trampoline. And you scream, 'RISE AND SHINE, YOU BUM!' And if he still doesn't

wake up, you squirt him with your juice box on his nose and toes."

"I see," said Dad. "Crude, but effective."

It is always nice when your dad is proud of you.

"Mom," I said. "What about the art stuff?"

Mom was using the toaster for a mirror. "I have bags under my eyes," she said.

I tugged on her sleeve.

Sometimes that helps moms focus.

"Mom," I said. "We need goo sticks and scissors and paper."

"*Glue* sticks," Mom said. "The art supplies are in the junk drawer. Would you get them, Roscoe? I need to see if Max is ready for school."

The junk drawer is one of my favorite off-limits places.

It's like a pirate treasure chest.

Only with no rubies.

I opened the drawer.

I looked inside.

Wow, I thought. *This drawer is full of cool stuff!*

And that's when all my trouble started.

5

Don't-You-Dare Glue

The junk drawer always has wonderful things in it.

Keys. Puzzle pieces. Paper clips. The head from one of Hazel's dolls.

I was playing brain surgeon the day that happened.

The patient died.

I pulled out the bag of art supplies.

I added three purple rubber bands to the bag.

And a Slinky that wouldn't slink anymore.

And the doll head.

You never know when you might need an extra head.

And then I saw something else in the drawer.

A bottle of Super-Mega-Gonzo Glue.

The grown-up glue Mom calls *don't-you-dare* glue.

Super-Mega-Gonzo Glue is extra strong.

Dad used it when I broke my great-grandma's very old teacup.

And when I broke Mom's very precious flower vase.

And when I broke Grandpa's very ugly glass potato souvenir from Idaho.

Adults really should keep breakable stuff away from us kids.

Mom glanced into the family room. "Max! Did you find your other shoe? The bus will be here in five minutes."

My big brother came into the kitchen.

He was armed with a juice box.

"My shoe is on the roof," Max said. Then he squirted me with his straw.

At least it was apple juice. That's my favorite.

"Max!" Mom cried.

"He started this war," Max said.

"My hair's all wet," I complained.

"Maybe you should cut off your head," Max said.

Which was not all that helpful, really.

"Shut up," I said to Max.

"Roscoe!" Dad said.

"Shut up, PLEASE," I said.

"Wait just a minute, Max," Mom said. "Did you say your shoe is *on the roof*?"

"There's a good explanation," Max said.

"I'm sure there is," said Dad. His eyebrow went up again.

That eyebrow gets a lot of exercise.

"Me and Roscoe were playing astronaut," Max said.

"Max's shoe was the space shuttle," I added.

"I need a ladder," Mom said.

"I need more coffee," Dad said.

"I need a new brother," I said.

"You need a new brain," said Max.

"Guys," said Dad. "Peace."

"Roscoe, Max and your dad and I have work to do on the roof," Mom said. "Keep an eye on Hazel for me, sweetie."

Hazel is my little sister. She was busy watching cartoons in the family room.

Mom says educational cartoons are okay.

Especially until she's had her first cup of coffee.

"I'll hold the ladder," Dad said to Mom, "if you climb."

Dad is afraid of heights. But don't tell anybody. It's a family secret.

Also, please don't tell him he is losing his hair.

Dads can be very sensitive, you know.

"Dad," I said. "Before you go outside, I think you should know you only have one sock on."

Dad looked down at his foot. "Has anyone seen my other sock?"

"Try the roof," Mom said.

"Try Goofy's stomach," I said. "I think he ate it."

Goofy is our big white dog.

He is very open-minded about his diet.

Dad groaned. Then he went outside with his one bare foot. Followed by Max and Mom.

I checked on Hazel. She was talking to a blue dog on the TV screen.

Goofy was eating her cereal.

I went back to the junk drawer.

I picked up the *don't-you-dare* glue.

I imagined Mom saying, "Roscoe, don't you dare touch the *don't-you-dare* glue!"

I put the glue down.

I imagined my teacher saying, "Roscoe, what a wonderful helper you are! Thank you so much for the grown-up glue!"

Hazel came into the kitchen. She was wearing a paper crown.

Hazel's favorite games are Princess Dress-up, Mud Pie Picnic, and Let's Dress Up Roscoe Like a Princess and Make Him Eat Mud Pies.

". . . h, i, j, k, Ellen Emmo peed," Hazel sang.

She paused. "Who is Ellen Emmo?" she asked.

"They'll explain all that in kindergarten," I said.

I picked up the glue again.

Hazel's eyes got big. "That's the *don't-you-dare* glue!"

"It's for my teacher," I said. "Things are
always breaking at school. Like yesterday,
when I broke the pencil sharpener."

Sometimes I get a little carried away
when I'm sharpening.

I put the glue in the bag of art supplies. Then I grabbed my Hero Guy backpack.

Hero Guy doesn't have his own TV show or anything.

Mom got him on sale at the mall.

"Hey, Roscoe," Max called. "Hurry up! The bus is coming! And you gotta come see something!"

I took Hazel's hand. I looked at the junk drawer one last time.

Maybe I should put the glue back, I thought.

After all, when you call something *don't-you-dare* glue, there's probably a good reason.

I could hear the bus driver honking.

Oh well, I thought.

It was just a harmless little bitty bottle of glue.

When Hazel and I got outside, I saw a big silver ladder leaning against the house.

Dad was holding it.

"Check it out!" Max exclaimed. "Mom's on the roof again!"

"Excellent," I said.

That is always a good way to start your day.

I yelled good-bye as I ran for the bus stop.

"See you at the open house!" Dad called.

Just then there was a big gust of wind.

The ladder fell with a crash.

Probably Mom would have yelled good-bye, too.

But she was too busy hanging from the roof.

6

The Secret Handshake

When I got to my classroom, my friends Gus and Emma ran over to say hello.

The first thing we did was our Secret Handshake.

Here is how it goes. In case you would like to try it.

1. Scream each other's names.

2. Wait for the teacher to say, "Inside voices, PLEASE!"

3. Do a high five.

4. Do a low five.

5. Stick out your tongue.

6. Get all serious and say, "How do you do, Mr. Riley?"

Of course, you would not say *Riley*, probably.

It would be pretty amazing if we had the same last name.

Emma pointed to my elbows. "Cool sparkle Band-Aids, Roscoe."

I mostly always have a Band-Aid on me somewhere.

Or a cast. Or a sling.

Mom says to think of it all as a fashion statement.

When I was four, I even had an eye patch.

The eye patch was black. Totally pirate.

"How'd you get the Band-Aids?" Gus asked.

"Racing my Hot Wheels car down the stairs," I said. "The Hot Wheels won."

"Household accidents are the most

common cause of injuries in children," said Emma.

Emma teaches me lots of interesting facts.

She was born in China. Her parents adopted her when she was a baby.

I wish I was born in China. Instead of just Kalamazoo.

Gus teaches me lots of useful things too.

Just last week he showed me how to make armpit farts.

"What's in the bag, Roscoe?" Emma asked.

"Art stuff for Ms. Diz," I said.

I opened the bag. Gus and Emma peeked inside.

"Cool head," Gus said.

"Her name was Drusilla," I said. "Before I brain-surgeried her."

"Super-Mega-Gonzo Glue!" Gus said. "Whoa. My mom won't let me near that stuff!"

"Me either," said Emma.

"Me either," I said. "But I figured Ms. Diz could use it. For when we break stuff. Let's go show her what I brought."

Ms. Diz was busy stapling butterfly pictures to the bulletin board.

Ms. Diz isn't really her name.

But her real name is hard to say. It uses maybe half of the alphabet.

So she cut off the end for my class.

Maybe when I'm a grown-up, I'll be called Mr. Ri for short.

Or not.

I handed Ms. Diz the bag of art supplies. "This is for you," I said. "It's for the art cupboard. There's special glue in there.

And I even included a free head."

Ms. Diz frowned. "What *kind* of head, Roscoe?"

"Just a doll head." I smiled so she wouldn't worry.

Since Ms. Diz is new, she gets mixed up sometimes.

I try to help her out whenever I can.

After all, I was a kindergartner last year. So I already know everything there is to know about school.

For example, when Ms. Diz forgot the janitor's name, I remembered it was Mr. McGeely.

She had to call him when Gus threw up his ravioli after lunch.

Sometimes Ms. Diz looks pretty pooped by the end of the day.

I hope she doesn't decide to go into

another line of work. My kindergarten teacher did that.

It wasn't my fault.

Probably.

Although I think maybe she got a little frustrated when I painted the class hamsters. Green. Because it was Saint Patrick's Day.

Hamsters like to look perky for the holidays.

Ms. Diz checked her watch. "Class!" she said in a loud voice.

Then she put a finger on her lips. That means SHHH.

"I know you're all excited about the open house today," said Ms. Diz. "We're going to have a dress rehearsal first thing this morning."

Dress rehearsal is when you practice

with costumes and stuff.

It doesn't mean you have to wear a dress.

"Let's just hope things go a little better than they did yesterday," Ms. Diz said with a laugh. "I'm sure today we'll all be on our best behavior."

Poor old brand-new Ms. Diz.

I think maybe she forgot about our high spirits.

7

Mess Rehearsal

"First, I want all you bees to put on your antennae," said Ms. Diz.

Real bees use their head bobbles to smell and feel things.

But ours were just made of pipe cleaners and Styrofoam balls. With glitter on them.

They were attached to a plastic headband thingie. Shaped like a great big upside-down U.

Last year the third graders used the bobbles for a play about butterflies.

So the headbands were a little stretched out by their gigantic third-grade heads.

When we were ready, Ms. Diz went to the music cupboard.

She handed each drummer two red tapping sticks.

We use the sticks for Music Time. They are our instruments.

Only really I would rather have a drum set.

Or a tuba.

"I know how much fun the sticks are, children," said Ms. Diz. "But as you may recall, some of you got a little carried away yesterday."

I think maybe she was looking at me.

But I wasn't the only one who got in stick trouble.

Gus was the one who started the pretend sword fight.

I was Not Guilty.

Mostly.

"Our rhythm section sits in the chairs," said Ms. Diz. "Nice and still."

That was me. And Gus. And Dewan and Maria and Coco.

"All the other bees in the back row," said Ms. Diz. "Standing up nice and tall."

We got into our places.

Bees and bee drummers.

Bobbles and sticks.

We were ready for action.

"Okay, let's sing nice and clear," said Ms. Diz. "And no poking with the sticks."

"How about swords?" Dewan asked.

"No swords," said Ms. Diz.

"How about death rays?" Gus asked.

"No death rays," said Ms. Diz. "When I count to three, start singing!"

Here is how our bee song goes:

Buzzy bees, fuzzy bees,
Look at us fly!
Bees are the best bugs!
You want to know why?
We make our own honey
and soar in the sky.
Can you do what we do?
We dare you to try!

"Great job!" said Ms. Diz when we were done. "Roscoe, you sound especially wonderful. But we need to hear the other kids too."

"He's blowing out my eardrums, Ms. Diz," Coco complained.

"My head bobbles keep falling off!" Wyatt said.

Ms. Diz took a deep breath.

"I know the antennae don't fit very well, children. Just do the best you can. Let's try the song one more time. This time, let me hear those sticks pounding out the rhythm!"

We sang again. I was not so loud this time.

But if you ask me, they were missing out.

"Better," said Ms. Diz when we were done.

"My bobbles

keep falling in my eyes!" Hassan said.

"Oh, dear," said Ms. Diz. "Maybe we should just forget about the antennae."

"But we have to have bobbles!" Coco cried. "Otherwise how will our parents know we're bees?"

"You make a good point, Coco. Hassan, bring me your antennae," said Ms. Diz. "Maybe I can tighten them up a little."

While Ms. Diz worked on Hassan's bobbles, Maria started tapping her sticks.

Dewan tapped along.

Gus tapped too.

On my head.

"Children," said Ms. Diz. She was

still trying to fix Hassan's bobbles. "No tapping, please."

We sat and waited. While we sat there, I came up with a new invention.

I put the rhythm sticks in my mouth.

I made them point straight down.

Ta-da! Walrus teeth!

I think when I grow up I may be a famous inventor.

Or else an ice cream truck driver.

Dewan and Gus laughed at my walrus teeth.

Maria put her sticks on her head. She looked just like an alien.

Even more people laughed.

Gus put his sticks up his nose.

He just looked gross.

Pretty soon we were all tapping and laughing and being walruses and aliens.

Except Gus.

He just kept the sticks in his nose.

"Children!" said Ms. Diz loudly.

But we couldn't hear her very well.

What with all the tapping and laughing.

Gus held up one of his nose sticks. "I challenge you to a duel!" he cried.

"Yuck," said Coco.

I jumped up on my chair.

So did Gus.

You can't sword-fight sitting down.

We sort of forgot about the no-sword-fighting rule.

"Roscoe!!! Gus!!! Children!!!" Ms. Diz held up her hand and put a finger to her

lips. "Quiet down NOW!"

We got very quiet.

Gus and I froze on our chairs.

Ms. Diz pointed to the doorway.

Mr. Goosegarden was standing there.

He is the principal. That is the big boss of the school.

He is mostly nice.

Unless you've been Making Bad Choices.

Then you have to sit in his office and think about your behavior.

When that happens, Mr. Goosegarden wears his I-mean-business face.

And right now, Mr. Goosegarden had on his I-REALLY-mean-business face.

8

How to Speak
Teacher

"Children," said Mr. Goosegarden. "I certainly hope you won't disappoint your parents with this kind of rowdy behavior at the open house."

Coco raised her hand.

"Roscoe started it, Mr. Goosegarden," she said. "He made walrus teeth."

Coco was not really being helpful.

If you ask me.

"I'm sure Roscoe will remember that walrus teeth are not appropriate," said Mr. Goosegarden. "And that chairs are for sitting. Not sword fighting."

He winked at me.

Mr. Goosegarden and I go way back.

"Sorry," I said. "I didn't know there was a no-walrus-teeth rule."

"That's okay, Roscoe," said Mr. Goosegarden. "I know you will come through this afternoon."

He smiled at Ms. Diz. "Don't worry," he said. "The first year of teaching is always the hardest."

Mr. Goosegarden waved good-bye. The door closed behind him.

Ms. Diz sighed.

She looked at the clock on the wall. "It's way past time for reading groups.

Let's take off the head bobbles. . . . I mean the *antennae*. Just do the best you can this afternoon."

She sounded sort of worn-out.

I felt bad about the walrus-teeth incident.

Like I said before, kids have so many rules to remember!

There are a gazillion things we are not supposed to do.

Who knew making walrus teeth was one of them?

. . .

After we put away the bobbles and sticks, we sat at tables for reading groups.

Reading is fun. But it can be very hard work.

You can get pretty thirsty trying to make those letters into words.

After I read four whole sentences, I

went to the water fountain to get a drink.

The fountain is next to the art cupboard.

Just then, Mr. Frisbee came in. He is a kindergarten teacher.

"May I borrow some chalk?" Mr. Frisbee asked Ms. Diz.

"Sure," said Ms. Diz. She opened the art cupboard. I could see the art supplies I'd brought.

Including Drucilla's head.

And the *don't-you-dare* glue.

Ms. Diz gave Mr. Frisbee a fresh box of chalk. "Here you go," she said.

"How was the dress rehearsal?" Mr. Frisbee asked.

Ms. Diz whispered something I couldn't hear.

Then she laughed. "At this rate, I'll be looking for another job soon!"

They both laughed.

But I was pretty sure it was worried laughing.

Maybe you are wondering how I could tell.

After all, teachers can be confusing.

Not as confusing as parents.

But still. Sometimes teachers have trouble expressing themselves.

Fortunately, I have served in preschool and kindergarten already.

Also Mommy and Me Music.

And Gymborama.

And my clay class, Pots for Tots.

So I am happy to explain teacher stuff to you.

Here is my Goof-Proof Roscoe Riley Teacher Translator:

I told you not to feed glitter to the goldfish.

Really, really SHHHH.

Take the Play-Doh out of your ear this instant!

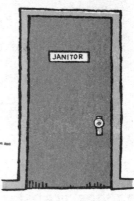

I quit. Just like the kindergarten teacher.

It's pretty easy to understand teachers. Once you get the hang of it.

I'm still working on figuring out how to speak Parent, though.

I thought about what Ms. Diz had said to Mr. Frisbee. *At this rate, I'll be looking for another job soon.*

What if Mr. Goosegarden fired Ms. Diz? Just because of our rowdy behavior?

That would be awful.

After all, Ms. Diz is a great teacher.

Even if she is just a beginner.

Then I thought about my kindergarten teacher from last year.

The one who changed jobs after I painted the hamsters.

She works at an office now.

With no kids in it.

And no green hamsters.

How boring is that?

I could not let such a horrible thing happen to Ms. Diz.

9

Roscoe to the Rescue

Right after recess, it was time to get ready for the open house.

Ms. Diz and the room mothers set out chocolate chip cookies and cakes and pies on a big table.

And napkins and juice.

Those cookies looked DELICIOUS.

But I was too worried about the bee song to think about those delicious, chewy, chocolaty, melt-in-my-mouth cookies.

Well, *almost* too worried.

Ms. Diz arranged the chairs. Then she set out the sticks and the head bobbles on the counter.

"Your parents will be here in just a few minutes, children," she said. "Check all the activity centers to be sure everything is nice and clean."

"Ms. Diz?" called one of the room mothers. "Do you have any name tags?"

"I think I have some in the art cupboard," said Ms. Diz.

She opened the cupboard doors. "Nope. No name tags. Let me see if they have any in the office. Children, I'll be right back. Roscoe, why don't you pass out the antennae? Dewan, you hand out the sticks. But no funny business. The rest of you finish cleaning up."

Ms. Diz rushed out the door.

The art cupboard doors were still open.

I could see the *don't-you-dare* glue I'd brought.

And just then I had a Super-Mega-Gonzo idea.

I went over to the cupboard.

All the kids were busy cleaning up blocks and puzzle pieces and crayons.

The room mothers were not paying attention to me, either.

They were busy mopping up a juice spill. It was caused by a flying LEGO.

I picked up one of the head bobbles on the counter.

I reached for the *don't-you-dare* glue.

I tried to read the label.

It took a LOT of work to read it.

Bonds instantly and permanently, it said. *Glues wood, metal, glass, and paper.*

The label did not mention head bobbles.

I opened the glue.

I put a little on the headband.

And I popped those bobbles on my head.

I waited a few seconds.

Then I wiggled my head.

The bobbles stayed on!

Nice and tight. Just like real bee bobbles.
Perfect.

I put a few drops of glue on all the other
bobbles.

Then I slipped the tube of glue into my
pocket.

One by one, I passed out bobbles to all
the kids.

Hassan tried on his bobbles.

He didn't notice the little drops of
don't-you-dare glue.

"Hey," said Hassan. He shook his head.
"Weird. My bobbles are staying on!"

"So are mine," Maria said. "Ms. Diz
must have fixed them."

I handed bobbles to Gus and Dewan.

They were playing swords again.

"Gus!" I said. "No swords! This open house has got to be perfect."

"They're not swords," he said. "They're lightsabers."

"Here," I said. I put the bobbles on his head.

And gave the last pair to Dewan, who put them on.

"Hey," said Dewan. "My bobbles aren't bobbling!"

Mission accomplished, I thought.

Roscoe to the rescue!

10

Bee-having

Ms. Diz came back with the name tags.

She was not happy to see Gus and Dewan playing swords again.

"Drummers, settle down," she said firmly.

"My bobbles are staying on, Ms. Diz," Maria reported.

"And so are mine," said Coco.

Ms. Diz looked surprised. "Hmm," she

said. "That's good news."

Just then Coco's mom and dad arrived. "Smile, everyone!" said her mom. "We're recording!"

Coco's dad was holding a silver camcorder.

All the other moms and dads began to come in.

They smiled and talked and waved and shook hands.

While Ms. Diz was busy saying hello, Gus pointed his stick at Dewan. "I am Zorro!" he yelled.

"I am Darth Vader!" cried Dewan.

"Duel to the death!" Gus shouted.

They were going to have a hard time sitting still for the bee song, I thought.

And then I had another Super-Mega-Gonzo idea.

Sometimes my brain amazes me.

I went over to the drummer chairs.

I looked around. Nobody was watching me. And Mom and Dad weren't there yet.

I pulled out the *don't-you-dare* glue. And I put a few drops on each chair seat.

I smiled a proud smile.

The bee song would go perfectly.

Ms. Diz would keep her job.

And all because of me.

"Roscoe! Hello, Pumpkin!" someone called.

It was Mom.

She was carrying her banana-avocado-raisin cream pie.

It is not really okay for moms to call you "Pumpkin" in front of your classmates.

But that's all right. Sometimes parents forget to follow the rules too.

My dad was right behind her.

He was carrying Hazel.

Hazel only goes to preschool half a day.

Little kids have it so easy.

"What's on Roscoe's head, Mommy?" Hazel asked.

"These are my bee bobbles," I said proudly.

I wiggled my head. They stayed put.

I am a genius, I thought.

Ms. Diz clapped her hands and put a finger to her lips.

"Parents, please find a seat. We have an exciting performance planned for you!"

All the moms and dads sat down.

They had to squish into our little bitty chairs.

They looked pretty silly.

I was glad no one tried to sit in the chairs I'd glued.

"Places, everyone," said Ms. Diz.

The bees lined up.

The bee drummers sat down.

Right on the glue.

All except Gus.

"There's something on my chair," he complained.

"Probably your own nose goo," said Coco.

"Gus," said Ms. Diz. "Please sit down."

Gus sighed. He sat down with a plop.

"As you may know, we've been studying insects these past few weeks," Ms. Diz said.

Suddenly Mr. Goosegarden appeared in the doorway.

"Hello, parents!" he said. "I'm just passing through. Didn't want to miss hearing my favorite beehive perform!"

Mr. Goosegarden looked at all of us.

One eyebrow went up.

Just like my dad's.

I wonder if there's a school where they learn that eyebrow move.

Ms. Diz made a noise with her throat. Her face was a little pink.

Or maybe green.

I think that's called stage fright.

"As I was saying," she said. "We've

been learning about insects. Especially bees. And now we have a song we'd like to perform for you."

Hazel made a buzzing sound.

All the parents laughed.

Everyone thinks she's adorable.

It's disgusting.

"All right, children," said Ms. Diz. She made her voice a whisper. "We are going to do this just right this time!"

She looked over at the drummers.

Even Gus was sitting perfectly still.

Not that he had a choice.

"One, two, three!" said Ms. Diz.

We all sang loud and clear. And pounded nice and steady.

When we were done, the parents cheered and clapped.

Someone even whistled.

"Bravo!" a dad yelled.

Coco's mom wiped tears from her eyes.

"Can we have cookies now?" asked Hazel.

Ms. Diz looked very happy.

And she wasn't pink or green anymore.

Mr. Goosegarden grinned. "Children, I knew you'd come through. That was just perfect. I must say that I loved the way you BEE-haved."

Everyone laughed at his bee joke.

Because you have to laugh when it's the principal.

Mr. Goosegarden gave Ms. Diz a thumbs-up sign.

That means GOOD JOB.

Also YOU WON'T HAVE TO GO WORK IN A BORING, HAMSTER-FREE OFFICE.

He gave us all a big wave.

And then he left.

I couldn't stop smiling. Everything had gone perfectly.

Thanks to me.

And a little bit of *don't-you-dare* glue.

"All right, everybody," said Ms. Diz. "Hand me your antennae and your sticks. And line up with your parents for dessert."

All the kids clapped and cheered.

Then everybody pulled off their head bobbles.

At least, everybody *tried* to pull off their head bobbles.

"Ouch!" Emma cried.

"The bobbles won't come off!" Dewan shouted.

"My hairs are pulling!" Gus yelled.

"MY BOBBLES ARE STUCK!!!" Coco
screamed.

Everybody looked at me.

Their faces were kind of surprised.

Then mad.

Then REALLY mad.

It seemed like maybe a good time for
me to go to the bathroom.

But when I tried to get up, my chair
came with me.

Uh-Oh

I yanked on that chair.

I tugged.

I pulled.

I whirled around like Goofy chasing his tail.

Gus and Dewan and Coco and Maria tried to get up too.

But those chairs were stuck to our clothes.

Permanently.

Just like the glue label had promised.

"Uh-oh," I said. Real softly.

No one heard me except Gus.

All the kids were too busy screaming about their bobbles.

And running around like crazy people.

Parents were dashing over to see what all the fuss was about.

Coco's dad was recording the whole mess.

And Ms. Diz looked a little like she might faint.

If you asked me, they were getting a little carried away about the head bobbles.

I mean, really, SOME of us had more important problems.

Like butt chairs.

"Roscoe," Gus said. "How come you said 'Uh-oh'? Did you do something?"

"The *don't-you-dare* glue," I whispered.
"I sort of dared."

"Whoa." Gus wiggled the chair attached

to his rear end. "That is SOME glue."

"I'm doomed," I said.

"Totally," Gus said.

Emma ran over to me. She was yanking on her head bobbles.

Just like everyone else.

"Roscoe," she said, "did you use the *don't-you-dare* glue on the bobbles?"

That Emma!

She knows me so well.

"ROSCOE RILEY!" Coco yelled. "THIS IS ALL YOUR FAULT! YOU ARE THE ONE WHO HANDED OUT THE BOBBLES!"

"Mommy!" Hazel said. "Is Roscoe going to time-out?"

"Roscoe?" Ms. Diz said.

"Roscoe?" said Mom.

"Roscoe?" said Dad.

I could hardly hear them.

What with all the screaming.

"Roscoe?" Ms. Diz said again. Louder this time. "Is there something you'd like to tell us?"

"What have you done to my Coco's beautiful head?" Coco's mom screamed.

I started to answer.

But just then Coco ran by.

Actually, Coco and her chair ran by.

"GET IT OFF OF ME!" she screeched.

That girl really has a great pair of lungs.

I tried to stop her so I could explain everything.

Only I sort of missed and grabbed one of her chair legs instead.

Coco lost her balance.

She tripped.

She did a way cool air somersault.

Right onto the dessert table.

All those beautiful desserts went flying.

Also Mom's horrible banana-avocado-raisin cream pie.

I watched that pie float through the air.

It was like a slow-motion movie.

Higher and higher.

Twirling and swirling.

A deadly missile made of bananas and avocados and raisins.

And it was heading straight for poor Ms. Diz.

I knew what I had to do.

After all the trouble I'd caused, I had to save my teacher.

I leaped into the air.

Which isn't easy to do when you have a chair attached to your butt.

SPLAT!!!!

That pie landed right in my face.

A direct hit.

Pie in my hair. On my clothes. On my bobbles.

I lay on the floor.

Chair glued to me.

Pie covering me.

Kids screaming.

Parents yelling.

But Ms. Diz was safe.

And you know, that pie really wasn't half bad.

12

Holes in Our Heads

Ms. Diz and the parents had to use scissors to cut us off our chairs.

That part was a little embarrassing.

Plus we had to borrow clothes from the lost-and-found box.

I had to wear pink bunny pants.

That part was WAY embarrassing.

They had to cut off our bobbles too.

We all lost a little hair.

Because of the glue situation.

Some of the kids were not too happy about the holes in their heads.

But I reminded them that their hair would grow back before they knew it.

I had to have a long talk with Ms. Diz and Mom and Dad.

When I explained to Ms. Diz how I was trying to save her job, she gave me a hug.

That is Teacher for *I forgive you, kiddo*.

She made me promise that next time I'd ask first before I tried to save her.

And to never, ever, ever touch *don't-you-dare* glue again.

She also said she loved her job.

And that Mr. Goosegarden would think the whole glue story was funny. Someday.

Like I said.

Ms. Diz is a great teacher.

Even if she is just a beginner.

13

Good-Bye from Time-Out

So now you know why I'm in time-out.

Actually, Mom and Dad were really proud of me for trying to help Ms. Diz.

They just didn't like the part where I took the *don't-you-dare* glue out of the drawer to begin with.

Now that I think about it, I can see

their point.

That glue is way sticky.

Anyway, thank you for hanging out with me.

It's been nice to have some company.

Here come Mom and Dad now.

I'm going to tell them again how sorry I am.

And then maybe we'll go to the barber shop to fix my bald spots.

Now I know how my dad feels.

But first we'll have a big hug.

That's the best part of time-out.

For Jessie and
her mom and dad

Contents

1

Welcome to Time-Out

Welcome to the Official Roscoe Riley Time-out Corner.

It's nice to have some company.

Getting stuck in time-out can be awfully boring.

Thing is, I got in a teensy bit of trouble. Again.

89

Even though I really, truly didn't mean to.

You know, it's hard for a guy like me to keep track of so many rules.

So I've started keeping a list.

This time I broke rule number 214: Do not kidnap your classmate's teddy bear.

And hide him in the dirty clothes basket.

Who knew?

You've bear-napped before, right?

Oh.

Bunny-napped? Pig-napped? Kangaroo-napped?

Oh.

Well, looking back, I guess it *does* seem like a bad idea.

But maybe you'll understand better if I tell you the whole story. . . .

Something You Should Know
Before We Get Started

You are never too old to love a stuffed animal.

I'll bet one of your favorite grown-ups has an old teddy bear hidden in a closet.

And I'll bet it has a silly name too.

Like Hugaboo. Or Mr. Tickletoes. Or Poopzilla.

Why do people always give their stuffed animals such crazy names?

Search me. I named my stuffed pig Hamilton.

He is way too cool to be called Poopzilla.

3

Something Else You Should Know
Before We Get Started

I don't care what you've heard.

Hamilton does NOT wear dresses.

4

Hamilton

I wouldn't be stuck here in time-out if I'd just listened to my big brother.

And believe me, I hardly ever say that.

It started the other day. I was packing Hamilton into my backpack.

So he could go to school with me. Just like always.

Max saw me. "No pigs allowed at school, Roscoe," he said.

I ignored him.

Because number one, that isn't a rule. Unless the pig is the real kind.

And number two, when a little brother ignores a big brother, it drives the big brother crazy.

Max was eating Cheerios. He threw one at my head. "You're in first grade now," he said. "And first graders do NOT take stuffed animals to school."

I picked the Cheerio out of my hair.

Then I ate it.

That also drives big brothers crazy.

"Hamilton always comes with me," I said.

Mom ran into the kitchen. "Has anyone seen Hazel's Cinderella toothbrush?"

Hazel is my little sister. She has a thing about princesses. Also mud.

"The point is, stuffed animals are for babies," Max said.

"Max!" Mom said. "What are you talking about?"

"Roscoe's taking that stinkpot Bacon to school," Max said.

"That isn't his name," I said.

"Ham," Max said.

"Ham-ILTON," I said.

"It would be totally embarrassing if anyone sees you with that thing," Max said. "I'd be humiliated!"

"You are in fourth grade," Mom said. "Roscoe's in first. How is he going to humiliate you?"

Max shook his head. "I'm sorry, Mom," he said, "but you know nothing about the real world. People will talk."

"That pig is Roscoe's best friend," Mom said. "And as long as it's okay with his teacher, he may take Bacon—I mean

Hamilton—to school."

"Besides, nobody knows he's there," I pointed out. "'Cause he stays in my backpack. Only Emma and Gus know about him. And Ms. Diz."

Ms. Diz is my teacher. And Emma and Gus are my best buddies.

Max made a pig-snort sound.

I snorted back. Twice.

Let me tell you, dealing with big brothers is an art.

"I'm bringing Hamilton," I said. "And that's that."

The thing is, I've had Hamilton forever.

My Great-aunt Hilda sent him to me on my first birthday.

She has a pig farm in North Carolina.

Great-aunt Hilda says pigs are very intelligent and lovable.

Sort of like snorting dogs.

I can't sleep without Hamilton.

When I was little, he kept away monsters and fire-breathing dragons.

When I got bigger, he kept away black widow spiders and grizzly bears.

He is my guard pig.

"Guys!" Dad called. "Hustle! It's almost time for the bus!"

Max ran to get his backpack. Mom ran to find Hazel's toothbrush.

I sat in the kitchen and stared at Hamilton.

I put him on the counter.

What if Max was right?

I was getting awfully old.

I mean, I had a loose tooth. That's WAY old.

Hamilton looked worried, like he might start to cry.

I could see this was very hard for him.

"Okay, buddy, you can come," I said.

I smushed Hamilton into the very bottom of my backpack.

I left the zipper open a little. So he could breathe.

Max was crazy. Nobody would bug me about Hamilton.

Because nobody knew about him. Except Ms. Diz and Emma and Gus.

I peeked into my backpack.

"Hamilton," I said. "You can come to school with me forever. Even when I'm a fourth grader."

5

Your Epidermis
Is Showing

When I got to school, I went straight to the cubbies by our classroom.

While I hung up my backpack, I checked to make sure no one was nearby.

Good. The coast was clear.

I whispered to Hamilton through the zipper hole. "See you, buddy."

I heard someone behind me. So I zipped up my backpack really quick.

My pal Gus ran up. His cubby is right next to mine.

Gus's cubby sign looks like this:

GUS CARR

My cubby sign looks like this:

ROSCOE RILEY

I have smaller letters on account of my name is longer.

We headed into the classroom. Emma ran over to join us.

Wyatt zoomed past us, pretending to be a jet.

"Hey, Gus," he yelled. "Your epidermis is showing."

Gus looked worried.

"*Epidermis* just means *skin*, Gus," I told him. "That is the oldest joke on the planet."

I know this because I have a big brother.

Max is useful for some things.

Wyatt zoomed back again.

"Hey, Roscoe," he said, "your proboscis is showing."

That was a new one. Even Max had never said it.

I checked for boogers. I checked my zipper. I checked every other embarrassing thing I could think of.

Emma made an I-don't-know-what-Wyatt's-talking-about face. And she knows lots of big words.

Wyatt laughed a loud, meanish laugh.

My dad says every classroom has a bully.

In Ms. Diz's class, his name is Wyatt.

Dad says when somebody like Wyatt teases you, a good answer is "So what?"

They never quite know what to say to that one.

This also works on little sisters and big brothers.

Feel free to borrow "So what?" anytime you need it.

"I see Roscoe's proboscis!" Wyatt yelled.

"So what?" I said.

Wyatt stopped zooming. He scrunched up his face.

"I'll bet you don't even know what that is," he said at last.

"Do so," I said.

"What is it then?" he said.

"Just zip it, Wyatt," said Emma.

That's a fancy way of saying BE QUIET.

Emma has a way with words.

Suddenly I remembered that I'd zipped up poor Hamilton. How would he breathe without an air hole?

"I'll be right back," I said.

I ran to the cubbies in the hall. No one was there.

I unzipped my backpack. So Hamilton could have some nice, fresh air.

I reached in to move him around. So he could be more comfortable.

"Now you look comfy," I said.

"Who are you talking to, Riley?" someone asked.

I smushed Hamilton down and spun around.

Wyatt!

"Nobody," I said. "I mean, I was just talking to myself."

Wyatt took a step closer. "What's in there, anyway?"

I could feel my face getting red. I hate that.

It's like your epidermis is tattling on you.

"I saw something," said Wyatt. "Is that a stuffed pig? Because stuffed animals are for loser babies."

"It's not a stuffed animal!" I cried. "It's a . . . a lunch bag."

"You talk to your lunch?" Wyatt asked.

"Only when it's bologna," I said.

Which I thought was a pretty good answer.

I walked back into class.

Wyatt was shaking his head.

And staring at my backpack.

6

The Case of the
Missing Pig

That night, after I brushed my teeth and put on my pajamas, I went down to the kitchen.

I grabbed my backpack off the counter. I reached inside to pull out Hamilton. But there was an empty space where Hamilton was supposed to be.

WHERE WAS HAMILTON????

I yelled. "HE'S GONE! HAMILTON IS GONE!!!"

Mom and Dad ran in. "Roscoe," Mom said, "what's wrong, honey?"

"HAMILTON IS MISSING I KNOW HE WAS IN HERE AND NOW HE IS GONE WHERE COULD HE BE???!!!" I screamed. "HAMILTON IS LOST!!!!"

I am not always calm in a crisis.

Not when it's about my pig.

"Can you think where you might have left him?" Mom asked.

"If I knew where I'd left him, then he wouldn't be lost!" I cried.

"Did you take Hamilton out for show-and-tell?" Dad asked.

"No way," I said. "Max said I would humiliate him if people knew I brought

Hamilton to school."

"So nobody saw you with the pig?" Max asked.

"Well," I said, "Wyatt saw me talking to him."

"I didn't know you spoke Pig," Max said.

I didn't answer. On account of I was ignoring Max.

"Wyatt is a real pain," I reminded Dad.

"Want me to talk to him?" Max said. "I could threaten to lock him in the boys' room."

"Max!" Mom said. "Don't even think such a thing!"

"A minute ago you were teasing Roscoe," said Dad. "And now you're trying to protect him?"

Max made his shoulders go up and

110

down. "It's my job, Dad. I'm his big brother."

We looked everywhere for Hamilton.

Under the couch. In the laundry room. In the toy chest. In the garage.

I even checked the bathtub.

Everybody tried to find Hamilton. Even our dog, Goofy.

He could tell we were looking for something.

So he brought us a slobbery tennis ball. A dirty sock. And a Lincoln Log he'd chewed on.

But no Hamilton.

Finally, Mom said, "I'm afraid we have to call it quits for tonight. Hamilton will show up, honey. He's just a very good hider."

We headed upstairs. I climbed into bed.

"My bed feels funny without Hamilton," I said.

Mom tucked the covers around me. "We'll find him, sweetheart," she said. "But for tonight, what could we do to make it easier to sleep?"

I stared at the ceiling. I have a mobile hanging there. It glows in the dark.

It's all the planets. Except Pluto. Which Goofy ate.

I guess that's okay. Since the science guys decided Pluto's not really a planet.

"There's nothing we can do," I said. "I can't sleep without Hamilton. Period. End of story. No more discussion."

Mom says that a lot.

You can pick up some really useful

sayings from adults.

Hazel came into my room.

She was wearing her Pretty Prancing Pony pajamas. With footies.

"Sweetie, you're supposed to be asleep," Mom said.

"I brought something for Roscoe," Hazel said. She held up one of her Barbie dolls.

The doll was wearing an astronaut helmet.

And a white doctor coat.

And purple sparkle high heels.

"Her name is Janelle," Hazel said.

She lay Janelle on my pillow.

It felt all wrong to see that sparkly astronaut doctor lying on Hamilton's favorite spot.

"You can borrow her," said Hazel. "Since you losted Hamilton."

"I didn't lose him!" I shouted. My voice was pretty grouchy. "He disappeared!"

"Roscoe, Hazel is just trying to help," Mom said.

I felt a little bad. Especially because Janelle is Hazel's favorite Barbie.

"Thanks, Hazel," I said. "You're a good sister." I picked up Janelle. Even though I really didn't want to.

She had pointy little hands.

Hamilton had nice soft piggy paws.

"Remember that Janelle likes to sleep with her high heels on," Hazel said.

She sounded a little worried.

"You know what?" I said. "I think Janelle would miss you." I handed Janelle back to Hazel. "She probably wouldn't be able to sleep. But thanks, Hazel."

Hazel grinned. "Yeah, you're probably right. Janelle is very picky."

Mom kissed the top of my head. "Sleep tight, Pumpkin. Hamilton will turn up, I'm sure of it."

After they left, I stared up at my glow-in-the-dark planets.

There was a big, empty spot next to me.

Right where Hamilton was supposed to be.

He snores a little, but that's okay.

Because all pigs do.

The planets swirled softly over my head.

Usually Hamilton and I loved to watch them.

But tonight all I could think about was Pluto.

The missing planet.

7

Pig-Napper!

"Roscoe, you look terrible," said Emma the next morning at school.

"REALLY terrible," Gus agreed.

"I had bad dreams all night," I said. "I dreamed I was a giant pig. And I got locked in a suitcase. And sent to Alaska."

"Alaska, huh?" Emma said.

"I think it was Alaska. 'Cause there

were polar bears and giraffes."

I felt my eyes getting wettish.

Which is not okay when you are an official first grader.

"I can't find Hamilton," I said. "I brought him to school yesterday just like always. And when I got home, he was vanished!"

"Wow," said Gus. "Pig-napping is a serious crime."

"Pig-napping?" I cried. "You mean someone stole him?"

"We don't know if he was pig-napped," Emma pointed out. "Maybe Roscoe left him somewhere. Did you take him to the boys' room?"

When you have a big problem, it is nice to have a good thinker like Emma around.

I shook my head.

"The lunchroom?" Emma asked.

I shook my head harder.

"Did you show him to anyone?" Emma asked.

I thought for a second. "Just Wyatt. I didn't mean for him to see us. But he did. Hamilton was in my backpack. I was just saying a quickie hi."

We all looked over at Wyatt. He was in the activity center making a magnet building.

He saw us looking at him. He pulled on his nose to make a pig face.

"Wyatt isn't my favorite person," Emma said. "He isn't even my tenth favorite person."

"Maybe Wyatt knows what happened to Hamilton," Gus said.

I thought about that. Wyatt was a meanie.

And he'd seen me with Hamilton.

And now Hamilton was missing.

"You don't think . . . Wyatt's a pig-napper, do you?" I whispered.

"Wyatt? Why would Wyatt pig-nap Hamilton?" Gus asked. "I was thinking maybe Mr. McGeely took him."

"Mr. McGeely?" I repeated. "You mean the janitor? You think Mr. McGeely put Hamilton IN THE TRASH?"

"No offense, Roscoe," Gus said. "But Hamilton is kind of, well, old."

"And he smells a little . . . funny," Emma added.

"My Great-aunt Hilda is old and smells funny, and I love her," I said.

Emma smiled. "You're a good guy, Roscoe."

"You know what I'm going to do?" I said. "I'm going to march right over there. And I'm going to ask Wyatt if he took my pig."

But before I could do that, Ms. Diz rang her gonger. It is a big round golden thing shaped like a plate. It hangs from a hook on the ceiling.

When you hit it with a hammer, it goes

g-o-o-n-n-g-g!!!

That means FREEZE!

Ms. Diz used to ring a teensy little silver bell.

But then she figured out we could make more noise than any old bell.

So she outsmarted us. With her giant gonger.

Ms. Diz is a brand-new teacher.

But she is learning fast.

"Time for morning meeting, folks," said Ms. Diz.

We sat in our spots.

We talked about the weather. (Cold.)

We talked about the day. (Tuesday.)

We talked about talking. (We had been

interrupting Ms. Diz a lot.)

She said that when someone is talking, you listen with your ears.

And save your questions for the end.

Then you use your mouth.

Even if you see something that is a miracle.

Like a squirrel with a blue Matchbox car in his mouth.

Which I saw yesterday.

You are not allowed to jump up and scream, "MS. DIZ I SEE A SQUIRREL WITH A MATCHBOX CAR IN HIS MOUTH OR MAYBE IT'S AN SUV!!! I AM NOT KIDDING MS. DIZ!!"

That's just a for-instance.

After we talked about the weather and the day, we read our morning message. Ms. Diz writes it on a giant piece of paper.

123

It said:

> We have art this afternoon with Ms. Large.
> Tomorrow is Hassan's birthday.
> Today Wyatt is our line leader.

I looked over at Wyatt.

He pulled up his nose to make another pig face.

That did it. I jumped up.

I put my hands on my hips. Like a superhero.

"WHAT HAVE YOU DONE WITH MY PIG?" I screamed.

Everybody froze. They were perfectly quiet.

So that when I also screamed, "YOU, SIR, ARE A PIG-NAPPER!" my very loud voice seemed extra especially loud.

"I AM NOT A PIG-NAPPER!" Wyatt screamed back.

He looked at Ms. Diz. "What's a pig-napper, Ms. Diz?"

"Roscoe and Wyatt!" said Ms. Diz. "First of all, sit down, please. Secondly, if you have something to say, you raise your hand."

I raised my hand. I waved it back and forth. Fast as Goofy's tail when he sees my mom with a can opener.

"Yes, Roscoe?" said Ms. Diz.

I looked at Wyatt. "You, sir, are a pig-napper," I said in a nice, gentleman voice.

Wyatt raised his hand. He waved it like a flag on a super windy day.

"Yes, Wyatt?" said Ms. Diz. She looked a little tired. And it was still morning.

"I am not a pig-napper," Wyatt said in a

nice, gentleman voice. "And what exactly is a pig-napper?"

"A pig-napper is a person who takes another kid's most favorite pig out of his backpack when he isn't looking!" I said.

Wyatt rolled his eyes. "Why would I want your stupid stuffed animal? Stuffed animals are for loser babies. I did not take your stinky pig!"

"Prove it!" I screamed.

"You prove it!" Wyatt said. "You 'cused me!"

I ran to Wyatt's cubby. I grabbed his backpack and came back extra fast.

"Roscoe," said Ms. Diz. "This isn't appropriate behavior."

Wyatt jumped up. He grabbed the other side of his backpack.

It said WYATT on it with a picture of a dinosaur.

Wyatt looked pretty mad. Kind of like the *Tyrannosaurus rex* on his backpack.

But I just knew Hamilton was in that backpack.

So I kept pulling.

Ms. Diz came over. She pulled on the backpack straps.

All the kids watched. It was like tug-of-war.

Three ways.

"Boys, let go," said Ms. Diz.

Ms. Diz was using her Listen-or-Else Voice.

Wyatt let go.

So did I.

Ms. Diz fell backward.

She landed—*plop!*—in her teacher chair.

The backpack flew into the air.

Something popped out.

Something stuffed.

But it wasn't Hamilton.

8

Bobo

There on the ground sat a dirty yellow teddy bear. With only one ear.

"BOBO!" Wyatt cried.

He grabbed that bear and hugged it.

"You said only babies have stuffed animals," I said.

"Loser babies," Gus pointed out.

Wyatt's face got very pink.

He dropped that old bear on the ground.

"That's my little brother's bear," Wyatt said, very fast. "I don't know how he got in my backpack!"

But I could tell Wyatt was fibbing.

He had hugged that bear like he really meant it.

. . .

After that we had to go to Mr. Goosegarden's office.

He is the principal. That means he talks to you about your Bad Choices.

I think he is also the boss of the teachers.

Maybe they have to talk to Mr. Goosegarden about their Bad Choices too.

Mr. Goosegarden has a very cool office.

He has a zillion windup toys on his desk.

There is a monkey who does a back-flip.

A caterpillar who tap-dances.

A gorilla who pounds his chest.

And teeth that chatter.

The secretary, Mrs. LaBella, led us into Mr. Goosegarden's office. While we waited for him to come in, I wound up the chattering teeth.

Wyatt wound up the gorilla.

We didn't talk to each other.

But we let the toys fight it out on the floor.

Mr. Goosegarden entered. He did not seem surprised to see the teeth and the gorilla fighting.

He sat down and rubbed his eyes and talked to us about our noisiness.

And about blaming someone without any proof.

And about Bobo and Hamilton.

"Boys," he said, "I'll tell you a little secret. I still have my old teddy bear." He smiled. "And sometimes I even sleep with him."

We were very quiet.

Since this was shocking news.

"No way," I said.

"No way," Wyatt said.

"Way," Mr. Goosegarden said.

Then he made us shake hands.

And pull the chattering teeth off the gorilla.

. . .

We walked back to class, Wyatt and me.

We didn't talk. Because I was still sure Wyatt had my pig.

Well, *pretty* sure.

Also because now everybody knew about Hamilton.

Of course, everybody knew about Bobo, too.

All the way back to our classroom, I thought about poor lonely Hamilton.

Who would tell him funny stories?

Who would rub his tummy?

Who would hug him when he was sad? Who else could have pig-napped him? Except Wyatt?

It was exactly the kind of thing a bullyish guy like Wyatt would do.

We got to the classroom door. Wyatt's backpack was in his hallway cubby.

Bobo's dirty ear was sticking out.

It wasn't fair for Wyatt to have his stuffed animal, when I didn't have mine.

We headed into the classroom. I sat down at one of the worktables.

Emma and Gus sent me sorry-about-the-principal-visit looks.

Ms. Diz rang her gonger.

"We've had some talk today about how

stuffed animals are just for little children," she said.

"Loser babies," Gus corrected.

"Thank you, Gus," said Ms. Diz. "Next time, please raise your hand first."

Ms. Diz went to the blackboard. She wrote:

STUFFED ANIMAL PARTY!

"I would like each of you to bring a favorite stuffed animal to school the day after tomorrow. I think you'll see that all of us have an animal who's very special."

"Even you, Ms. Diz?" Moira asked.

"Even me." Ms. Diz smiled. "And Mr. Goosegarden."

All the kids laughed. Except me.

"Roscoe, I know that you'll be missing

Hamilton if he hasn't turned up by then,"
Ms. Diz said. "But do you have some other
special animal you could bring?"

I sighed. "If I can't have Hamilton, Ms.
Diz," I said, "then I don't want anyone."

I looked over at Wyatt.

He and Bobo were going to have fun
together at the party.

While I would be sad and lonely. And
so would Hamilton.

It wasn't fair.

Then I had an idea.

I wasn't going to be the only person
without his favorite stuffed animal.

9

Welcome to the Dirty Clothes Basket

All day long my tummy felt throw-uppy.

Like it does when we go on a family trip. And there are twisty roads.

I hardly ever actually throw up.

But I make the other people in the car pretty nervous.

When Max and me got off the bus,

Mom was in the yard with Hazel.

"How was school, Max?" Mom asked.

"Okay," he said.

"How was school, Roscoe?" Mom asked.

"Okay," I said.

"What did you do today?" Mom asked.

"Nothing," Max said.

"I did nothing too, Mommy," said Hazel, who just goes to preschool half a day.

"What did you do, Roscoe?" asked Mom.

"Nothing," I said.

Because that's what you always say.

Except secretly I was thinking, *Nothing, unless you count bear-napping*. Which is what I did during lunch when no one was looking. I had grabbed that old bear out of Wyatt's backpack and stuck him into mine.

I took off my backpack. I'd left the zipper open halfway.

One little black eye was staring at me.

One little black, mad, sad eye.

Just then, I remembered about the party.

"Ms. Diz is making us have a stuffed animal party the day after tomorrow. So we can see that animals aren't just for loser babies," I said.

"Maybe you could bring Geraldo," Mom said.

"I thought about that," I said. "But if Hamilton can't come, then I'm not bringing anybody else. If he found out, it would hurt his feelings."

I took my backpack to my room.

Bobo looked all squished. Plus he had some peanut butter on his right paw.

"I'm really sorry about this, Bobo," I said. "It's only for a little while."

I sat on my bed. Bobo leaned on my pillow.

He was not smiling at all.

He looked sort of down in the dumps.

"See, your owner took my pig," I said to Bobo. "At least, I'm pretty sure he did. And so if I take you, then Wyatt will see how I feel and then he'll give Hamilton back and then I'll give you back."

I tucked Bobo under the covers.

All of a sudden I thought of Mom tucking me in.

She would see Bobo. And she would ask me where he came from.

"Roscoe," she would say, "I don't believe I've met this guy."

I would have to admit I was a bear-napper.

And I was almost positive for sure that Mom would not approve.

I pulled Bobo out of bed.

I searched around my room for a good hiding place.

I put Bobo in my dirty clothes basket. All kinds of things like to hide in there.

Right under my very muddy jeans.

Hazel and I were playing dinosaur digger-upper that day.

Bobo peeked one sad eye out from under my jeans.

Plus his one ear.

He was lonely. I could tell.

It was hard to figure how he could miss that mean old Wyatt.

I got my armadillo, Geraldo. He was napping under my bed.

"Bobo," I said, "allow me to introduce Geraldo."

I tucked Geraldo in next to Bobo.

I closed my closet door.

At least Bobo would have some company tonight.

Unlike me and Wyatt.

10

Plum

When I woke up the next morning, there was a wet Wheaties flake on my nose.

Max was standing by my bed. Holding a bowl of cereal.

He tossed another Wheaties flake at me.

I sat up and ate it.

"Dad told me to wake you up," Max said.

I yawned. "I couldn't sleep last night."

"How come?" Max asked.

I pointed to my closet. "I think maybe there's a ghost in there," I said.

"Cool," Max said. He slurped down more cereal.

"Max," I said, "did you ever do anything bad so that something good would happen?"

"Sure," Max said. "But the bad part always catches up with you. And then Dad and Mom make you sweep out the garage as punishment."

I pulled the covers over my head. Sometimes big brothers really are right about stuff.

Max yanked all the covers off me.

Sometimes big brothers are right. But mostly they're just really annoying.

· · ·

At recess I didn't feel like playing.

Even though Gus found a dead toad with its guts gooing out.

Which usually I wouldn't want to miss, of course.

I sat on a swing. But I didn't actually swing.

Down on the other end of the swing set,

Wyatt was also not swinging.

Ms. Diz came over. She was wearing a pink-and-green scarf.

"Look at you two," she said. "You both seem awfully glum."

"Plum?" I repeated.

"Glum," Ms. Diz said. "Sad."

"I miss Bobo," Wyatt said. "When I got home yesterday, he was missing from my backpack. Just like Hamilton!"

"I miss Hamilton," I said back.

I gave him a look that said *pig-napper*.

"My goodness," said Ms. Diz. "We're having quite an epidemic of disappearing animals!"

She looked at me. Then she looked at Wyatt.

Then she looked at both of us and shook her head.

Wyatt just sat there.

He didn't even have the heart to say a mean bully thing.

He looked like I felt.

Which was awfully plum.

• • •

The next morning was party day.

But I was not feeling at all party-ful.

I still did not have Hamilton back.

And I still *did* have Bobo.

"Roscoe?" Mom said as I headed out

the door. "Are you sure you don't want to bring Geraldo to school today?"

"Nope," I said. "Armadillos are not really party animals, Mom."

As we walked toward the bus stop, I heard Max calling my name.

"Hey, Roscoe," he yelled. "Heads up!"

I turned around. Something blue and floppy was flying through the air.

I caught it.

It was a blue, dirty, droopy dog.

"Who's this?" I asked. "He looks kind of familiar."

Max ran up to join me. "That's my dog. Blueberry."

He unzipped my backpack. "Quick, put him in here before the bus comes."

I squinted my eyes. "Wait a minute. You said you don't have a stuffed animal."

Max shrugged and said, "Roscoe, Roscoe, Roscoe. When are you going to learn? You should only believe your big brother half the time."

"Thanks, Max."

I tried to give him a hug. He yanked away.

"Bus, Roscoe," Max said. "Where's your pride, kid?"

I opened my zipper. "So he can breathe," I explained.

Max grinned. "You're all right," he said. "For a weenie."

• • •

Blueberry fit in with all the other animals.

Emma brought her gorilla.

Gus brought a stuffed snake. It was maybe six feet long.

Wyatt brought a white bunny. He said

he borrowed it from his brother.

That bully boy still looked pretty sad.

Ms. Diz even brought a stuffed animal. It was a kangaroo. And was that guy ever old!

He had patches. He was missing one eye. And his tail was all tattered. From a bad washing machine experience.

Mr. Goosegarden showed up with his old stuffed bear.

We sat in a circle and told about our animals.

Everybody looked a little embarrassed at first.

But before long we were all having fun.

It made me sad to think that Hamilton was missing out.

He loves a good party.

I had a feeling Wyatt was missing Bobo, too.

It turned out we all had favorite animals.

We slept with them.

And drooled on them.

And told them our troubles.

Because whether they were snakes or dogs or teddy bears or porcupines, they were all very good listeners.

11

A Very Unusual Football

"Cheer up, Roscoe," said Emma on the bus that afternoon.

"I'll bet Hamilton is just playing hide-and-seek," said Gus. "A really, really long game of hide-and-seek."

Some kids in the middle of the bus were throwing a football back and forth.

"No throwing things!" shouted the bus driver.

"Or maybe he went on a trip," said Emma.

"Yeah," said Gus. "Maybe he's flying around the world. He could be anywhere by now!"

I sighed.

The ball flew past us.

It was big and pink. And fluffy.

It was for sure not a football.

"Touchdown!" yelled one of the kids.

"No football on the bus!" yelled the driver.

"That's not a football," Emma pointed out. "It's fuzzy. And it's wearing a dress."

I looked.

I swallowed.

I jumped right out of my seat.

Even though that's a really bad idea on a bus.

"THAT'S NOT A FOOTBALL! THAT'S MY PIG!!!" I screamed.

The throwing stopped.

The kids stopped.

The BUS stopped.

"Excuse me?" said the driver.

"HAMILTON!!!" I ran over as fast as I could.

A little boy was holding him. A kindergartner.

"Here," he said. "You can have him. Truth is, he kind of smells, you know?"

"He's wearing a dress!" I cried.

Poor Hamilton. He looked so embarrassed.

"We thought he was a girl," the boy said.

I hugged that pig and I kissed that pig

and I didn't care who saw me.

Then I took off his dress.

I saw Max at the back of the bus. He was shaking his head. And laughing with his friends.

His friends who were way too cool to have stuffed animals.

Then Max looked right at me.

And he gave me a wink that only I could see.

. . .

My dad was working in his attic office when I got home.

I ran straight upstairs and told him the amazing wonderful story of Hamilton's return.

"This little girl found him on the sidewalk!" I said.

"The sidewalk?" Dad said.

"I think maybe he fell out of my back-pack when I was doing somersaults on the way home," I said. "Like this."

I did a quickie somersault example.

I kind of knocked into Dad's trash can.

"Oops," I said. "So the girl said she took Hamilton home. And she named him Darlene."

Dad shook his head. "Poor Hamilton."

"And her mom said Hamilton smelled bad. So she put him in the washing machine. Can you believe it?"

"That must have been scary for Hamilton," Dad said.

"So then the girl put a dress on him. Only her mom said he was still too yucky. Which he is not."

I took a whiff of Hamilton.

He still smelled sort of piggy-flavored.

But soapy too.

I hoped the soapy smell would wear off.

"So then the girl gave Hamilton to her brother to use as a football," I said.

I took a deep breath.

"Period," I said. "End of story. No more discussion."

But it wasn't, not really.

12

Your Proboscis Is Showing Too

I took Hamilton to my room so he could see all his friends.

Everyone wanted to hear his exciting story.

I grabbed Geraldo from my laundry basket so he could welcome his buddy back.

I started to close the closet door. But

something made me stop.

And it wasn't a ghost.

I looked down at the laundry basket.
Two sad black eyes
stared up at me.
Hamilton
and I were
together again,
but Bobo was
still alone.

And I knew
that wasn't right.

. . .

I told Dad all about how I had bear-napped poor Bobo.

It felt good to get that old bear off my chest.

Then Dad and I drove over to Wyatt's house.

On the way, Dad and me talked about jumping to conclusions.

Jumping to conclusions isn't about the fun kind of jumping. Like jumping rope. Or jumping jacks.

Jumping to conclusions is when you decide something before you know all the facts.

Like for instance when you think someone is a pig-napper.

Only they aren't.

We also talked about how you are

162

innocent until somebody proves you guilty.

Personally, I can see how that idea might come in handy.

Wyatt sure was happy to see Bobo.

I told him I was really sorry I thought he was a pig-napper.

And really sorry I was a bear-napper.

Before I left, I remembered something important I had to ask. "Wyatt?" I said. "What's a proboscis?"

"It's just another name for *nose*," he said. He grinned. "I learned it from my big brother. They're good for some things."

Wyatt gave Bobo a hug. Then he sniffed him.

He squinted his eyes. "You didn't give him a bath, did you?" he asked.

"No!" I said. "I might be a bear-napper. But I would never go that far!"

I sighed. "Somebody did that to Hamilton. They even put a dress on him."

Wyatt shook his head. "Some people have no shame."

13

Good-Bye from Time-Out

So now you know why I'm in time-out.

I broke a rule. Number 214 on my list.

Do not bear-nap.

I also learned that sometimes when people say they're Not Guilty, they might *really* be Not Guilty.

Even if their name is Wyatt.

And I learned what a proboscis is.

One more thing. I learned that it's okay to have a stuffed animal. Even if you're twenty, or sixty-five, or one hundred and one.

It's nice to have someone around who always understands you.

That's why I have Hamilton with me here in time-out. He knows I'm really sorry about all the trouble.

Here come Mom and Dad.

They know I'm sorry too.

I think I'll ask them if they still have any stuffed animals.

If they don't, I just might loan them one of mine.

Just as long as it's not Hamilton.

He's had enough adventures lately.

For Julia and Jake,
with love

Contents

1

Welcome to
Time-Out

Hey! Want to play?

Oops. I mean, want to play when I'm done with time-out?

I sort of kind of got in some trouble again.

'Cause I sort of kind of borrowed

somebody's dog.

I only borrowed him so I could win a trophy.

A shiny, sparkly, silver trophy.

You've probably borrowed a dog before, right?

A cat? A gerbil? A tarantula?

Oh. Well, I had my reasons.

It's a long story, actually.

Usually when I end up in time-out, there's a long story to tell.

And since you're here anyway, I'll bet you'd like to hear it. . . .

2

Something You Should Know
Before We Get Started

Just because your dog cannot read a book does not mean he isn't a winner.

Maybe he just hasn't figured out his real talent yet.

3

Something Else You Should Know
Before We Get Started

If your grandma knits you a sweater with pandas and smiley faces and hearts and baby ducks on it, do not give it to Martin.

Or anybody else.

It has sentimental value, you know.

4

The World's Best Roscoe Riley

This all started because my little sister won another trophy.

Hazel is still in preschool. And she already has a golden trophy from Little Minnows swim team. And one for being the Fastest Skipper in Ms. MacNamara's pre-K class.

So you can see why I was the teensiest bit annoyed when she came home with *another* trophy.

I'd had a long, hard day at school.

On account of an incident involving chocolate milk.

Did you know that if you blow through a straw into chocolate milk, the bubbles will volcano right out of your cup?

The bubbling part is way cool.

Cleaning up the mess afterward is not so cool.

Anyway, after all that, I didn't need to hear Hazel's big news as soon as I opened the door.

"Roscoe!" she screamed. "I wonned another one! For bestest sitting-stiller for the month at circle time!"

"I never got a trophy, and I sit still," I

said. "Well, sometimes I do."

Life is so not fair.

I dropped my backpack in the hall. I kicked off my tennis shoes. Then I flopped on the couch.

"You will not be getting any trophies for neatest boy on planet Earth," Mom said.

"Backpack in the closet. Shoes in your room." She kissed the top of my head.

"I want a trophy," I said in that whining voice you use when you feel really sorry for yourself.

"You got that little plastic statue in kindergarten last year," Mom said. "For most improved hand raising."

"I mean a *real* trophy," I said. "A big, heavy one. Made of gold."

"Shoes," Mom said. "Backpack."

I got off the couch and picked up my shoes and my backpack.

"You are the best burper in first grade," my big brother Max said.

He burped an extra loud one.

It was beautiful. Like music.

"But I'm still the best in the world," Max added.

Which is true. My brother has a gift.

"Everybody's got something cool like a trophy or a statue or something to take to show-and-tell," I said.

"*Every*body?" Mom asked.

"Last week Gus brought his yellow belt from karate," I said. "He got a little gold trophy cup with it. And today Emma brought her piano statue. She got it for practicing lots. It's of that grouchy guy."

"Ludwig van Beethoven," said Mom. "He was a famous music writer."

"Even you have a trophy, Mom," I said. "For selling Girl Scout cookies."

"That was a very long time ago," Mom said. "I was a great little salesperson, though. I could sell snow to a polar bear. I could sell water to an otter. I could sell—"

"Gee, Mom," I interrupted. "You are

big-time not helping me feel better. Which is sort of your job, after all."

Mom gave me a hug. "Sorry, sweetheart. You just be the very best Roscoe you can be. That's all that matters."

Easy for you to say, I thought. *You have a cookie trophy.*

Nobody gives a trophy for being The World's Best Roscoe Riley.

5

The World's Ugliest Sweater

"Don't forget Emma and Gus are coming over for a playdate," Mom said after I put my stuff away.

"Mom," I said with a groan, "we are not having a playdate. Hazel has playdates. We are hanging out."

"Well, when they get to the house for the

hang-out, please wear your new sweater if you go outside," Mom said.

"I will never wear that sweater," I said.

I crossed my arms over my chest. To show I meant business.

"Your grandmother knitted that sweater with her own two hands," Mom said.

"It has hearts on it! And flowers! And smiley faces! And baby ducks!" I cried.

"No sweater," Mom said, "no hang-out with Gus and Emma."

She tossed me the sweater. I put it on.

One side dangled down to my knees.

There was a pink bunny on the right sleeve. I hadn't noticed him before.

"NO!" Max cried. He covered his eyes. "Not the sweater of doom!"

Hazel wrinkled up her nose. "Why is there a monkey on the elbow?"

"That's a puppy," Mom said. She frowned. "At least, I think it is."

"Goofy and I are going to wait for Gus and Emma on the front porch," I said. "Cross your fingers nobody sees me."

"It was knit with love," Mom said. "It has sentimental value."

"What's mentisental value?" I asked.

"*Sentimental value* means you have to pretend to love your sweater when Grandma's here," Max said.

"*Sentimental value*," said Mom, "means that a gift is special to you because it came from someone you love."

I went outside. Goofy came with me.

He is a big, whitish guy dog with floppy ears.

His tail is usually in high gear.

And he almost always has something

in his mouth.

Right now he had Mom's cell phone.

"Not a good idea, Goofy," I said.

I went back inside and gave Mom the wet cell phone.

When I returned to the porch, Emma's dad dropped off Gus and Emma.

Gus and Emma live on the same street. It's a few blocks away from my house.

I wish I lived near them. Then we could be neighbors and best friends. Which is

very nice for hang-outs.

They ran over to the porch. Goofy licked their hands and wagged his tail extra speedy.

Then he licked one of Gus's sneakers for a while.

"You look kind of down in the dumps, Roscoe," Emma said.

"My sweater's ugly," I said. "And also I don't have any trophies and stuff like you guys."

Emma thought. "I would call your sweater interesting."

"I would call it very interesting," Gus said. "Why is there an armadillo on your shoulder?"

"That's a cow," I said.

"No," said Emma. "I'm pretty sure that's a kangaroo."

"COULD WE STOP TALKING ABOUT MY SWEATER?" I demanded.

Gus grinned. "Maybe you could get a blue ribbon for World's Weirdest Sweater."

I gave him my extra scary look.

"Okay, okay. No more sweater talk," he said.

"You know," said Emma, "it's never too late to get a trophy or a medal for something. You could learn to be a rodeo rider. Or an Olympic high diver."

Goofy started chasing his tail. He spun in crazy circles. He looked like a big white doughnut.

"Maybe Goofy could win a trophy for Best Tail Chaser," Gus said.

Goofy slammed into a bush.

"Or not," Emma added.

6

Jump, Frog, Jump!

We decided to play fetch with Goofy in the front yard.

We threw lots of tennis balls. Sometimes Goofy brought them back.

But mostly he just chewed them.

He even got three balls in his mouth at once.

He had a big, hairy clown smile.

When a boy walked by with his dog, Goofy ran over to say hello.

The dog was a little white poodle. He was wearing a silly doggie sweater with kitties on it.

"Sit, Edward," the boy said to the poodle.

Edward sat down. He did not move. He looked like a puffy statue.

Goofy raced around Edward in crazy circles. He barked. And sniffed.

And barked some more.

He looked goofy.

"I'm Martin," the boy said. "I just moved here a couple weeks ago. We used to live in Alaska."

"Did you live in one of those ice cube houses?" I asked.

"He means an igloo," Emma said.

Martin laughed. "Nope. Just a regular old house."

"Yeah," Gus said. "We live in regular old houses, too."

Martin pointed to my sweater. "Is that a poodle on your shoulder?"

"We're still trying to figure that out," I said.

"I really like animals," Martin said. "It's

a cool sweater."

I waited for him to laugh. But he didn't.

"I'm Roscoe," I said at last. "And that's Gus and Emma."

"Shake hands, Edward," Martin said.

Edward held up his paw.

Gus shook it. Emma shook it. I shook it.

Goofy licked it.

"Say hello, Edward," Martin said.

"Arf-arf," Edward said.

It was not exactly "hello," but you could tell what he meant.

"Wow! Your dog is amazing," said Emma.

"I was going to enter him in the Truly Terrific Trick Contest this weekend," Martin said. "But I have a tuba lesson."

"Do you mean the contest at the street fair?" Emma asked. "I saw a poster for that. Kids and their dogs can enter. And the winner gets a trophy."

"A trophy?" I asked. "Really?"

"Do they have a prize for Stupidest Pet Trick?" Gus asked. "I'll bet Goof could win that one!"

Goofy lay on his back on the sidewalk. I think he was ignoring Gus.

"What's your dog's name?" Martin asked.

"Goofy," I said. It sounded kind of lame next to a name like *Edward*.

Goofy wriggled on his back like a snake. His tongue was hanging out.

"What's he doing?" Martin asked.

"Itching," I said.

"Edward is never itchy," Martin said. He reached into his backpack. "Watch this."

Martin took out a book. "Just a regular

book, right?" He showed it to me. "Now read it."

"I've already read that," I said.

"Not you," Martin said. "Edward."

I laughed. "Your dog cannot read!"

"Why not?" Martin asked.

"Because he is a dog," I said. I said it very slowly and clearly.

Since apparently Martin was a little crazy.

"Just watch," Martin said.

He put the book on the ground. It was called *Frog on a Log*.

"Open the book, Edward," said Martin.

Edward put his little white poodle paw on the book.

He pulled on the cover.

The book flipped open.

"Good dog, Edward," Martin said.

"Now read to Roscoe."

Edward looked at the first page. So did I.

It said:

Frog on a log
in a big, dark bog.

Edward said:

Arf arf arf arf
arf arf arf arf arf.

"Good dog, Edward," said Martin. "Next page."

Edward turned the page with his nose. I looked over his shoulder.

The page had three words:

Jump, frog, jump!

Edward said:

Arf arf arf!

I looked at Martin.
I looked at Edward.

He didn't look so silly anymore. Even with the kitty sweater.

"That dog is a genius," I said.

We looked at Goofy.

He was eating an old gym sock.

"Your dog is nice too," Martin said.

7

Pandas

I thought about Edward and that book all the next day.

Especially when it was reading time.

Gus and Emma and I are in the same reading group. There are six kids.

All the groups have animal names. There are Panthers. Giraffes. And Tigers.

Gus and Emma and I are Pandas.

We each read two pages out loud.

When someone else is reading, we have to follow the rules:

1. No talking.
2. No laughing if somebody makes a mistake.
3. No sound effects.

Ms. Diz made up the third rule after we read our last book.

It was called *Honk! Honk! Beep! Beep!*

When we were all done, I asked Ms. Diz a question. I'd been wondering about it ever since meeting Edward.

"Ms. Diz," I asked, "do you think a dog can read?"

Ms. Diz thought for a second.

"Well, I doubt it, Roscoe," she said.

"Why do you ask?"

"Because Gus and Emma and me met a dog who could read *Frog on a Log*."

"He wasn't exactly reading, Roscoe," Gus said. "It was more like weird barking."

"But he barked when there was an actual word," I said. "If we can learn to read, why can't a dog?"

"Well, Roscoe," Ms. Diz said, "it's not that simple. Before you can read, you need to know your letters and the sounds they make. I've never met a dog who could do that."

"I'm telling you, Edward was reading," I said.

Sometimes, even when I'm not for-sure right, I kind of get stuck acting like I'm right.

I was feeling a little bit sticky at the moment.

Even Gus didn't think Edward was a reader.

And Gus believes everything.

I mean, Gus believes toads give you warts.

And everybody knows that's not true. Toads are great.

Frogs give you warts.

"I'll bet you dogs can read," I said. "I'll bet I could teach Goofy."

"Roscoe," Emma said, "I love Goofy. But he sits when you say *fetch*."

"And he lies down when you say *sit*," Gus added.

I know they weren't trying to be mean.

But I felt like I had to defend my dog.

"Goofy can learn anything!" I said. "He could win that dog trick contest if he wanted to!"

My mouth said all that real fast.

While my brain was still trying to catch up.

I hate it when that happens.

8

Roscoe Riley, Superteacher

Maybe you think it's easy being a teacher.

I used to.

After all, they get to boss around little kids all day.

How hard could that be?

Well, here are some things you should know in case you ever become a teacher:

204

1. Do not grouch at your students. Even if they stop their learning so they can chew their tail.

2. Do not try to make them learn everything in one day.

   On account of their brain might explode.

   Or they might take a nap.

3. Don't forget to praise your students when they do something right.

   A treat is a good idea.

   A cookie for the teacher is always nice, too.

I might even have given up teaching when my student tried to eat a book.

That can be pretty hard on a teacher.

But I kept seeing a beautiful picture in my head.

It was me at the dog trick contest. With Goofy by my side.

And a judge handing me a gigantic trophy.

The contest was Saturday. And today was Wednesday.

I didn't have a lot of time to teach Goofy to read like Edward.

The first thing I had to do was find the right book for Goofy.

I let him come with me to my bedroom. In case there was a book he especially liked.

For example, I like to read about dinosaurs. Also superheroes.

I found some books about dogs. (Because Goofy is one.)

And cars. (Because he likes to ride in them.)

And cats. (Because he likes to chase them.)

I put them on the floor in front of Goofy.

"Which one do you like, Goof?" I asked.

He didn't answer.

He was sniffing a dirty shirt on the floor. It had a nice, tasty spot of dried spaghetti sauce on it.

I picked a book called *Bad Cat Goes to the Vet*.

I figured Goofy would get a kick out of that.

We went to the kitchen. I stuffed my pockets with dog treats. And grabbed a banana for me.

"Where are you two going?" Mom asked.

"I'm teaching Goof to read," I said.

"After that, could you teach him to do

the dishes?" she asked.

As soon as we got outside, Goofy saw Hector.

Hector is a squirrel who lives in a big oak tree behind our house.

He loves to tease poor old Goofy.

Hector made some "Come and get me, doggie!" sounds.

Goofy flew across the yard.

His ears were flapping. His tongue was flapping.

Hector waited.

And waited.

And waited.

When Goofy was just a couple feet away, Hector zipped up his tree.

He made some more noises that said, "You moron! Why don't you ever learn, dogface?"

Goofy stared up at him, panting.

"You almost had him this time, guy," I said.

I always tell him that.

I went over to the other side of the yard. Away from Hector.

That's another thing about teaching. It's hard to get anything done if your

student is busy trying to eat a squirrel.

"Goofy!" I called. I peeled my banana. "Come! Time to read."

Goofy saw the banana.

I forgot how much that guy loves fruit.

He dashed across the yard.

He leaped up into my arms. I fell backward.

And we just kept rolling.

And rolling.

And rolling.

Man, was that fun!

We lay on the ground. Goofy licked my face.

I gave him the whole banana.

While he ate, I grabbed my book about Bad Cat.

"Today we are going to learn to read," I said. "First I will go."

I read nice and slow:

> Bad Cat chases Big Rat.
> Big Rat chases Bad Cat.
> Poor Bad Cat!
> Big Rat bit his tail.
> Bad Cat must go to the vet.

"Your turn," I said.

Goofy tried to eat the banana peel.

He looked at me with his big, happy eyes.

I could tell he wanted to understand.

But he couldn't quite figure me out.

I remembered feeling that way when I first learned to read.

Ms. Diz would point to a word like DOG.

And all I would see was ♣☆◇.

So I knew how Goofy felt.

I gave him a nice ear-scratch.

"We'll try again tomorrow, Goof," I said.

But he wasn't listening.

Hector was back.

9

The Swap

For the rest of the week, I worked with Goofy.

He did not learn any letters.

Or any words.

None.

But we had fun chasing Hector and rolling around together.

Even though it had nothing to do with reading.

On Friday I sat on the front steps with Goofy.

I had on my Grandma sweater. Because Mom made me wear it. Again.

Mom was mulching the garden.

Mulch is kind of like dirt. Mom says when she puts it around the plants, it's like giving them a blanket.

But if you ask me, a blanket shouldn't smell like cow poop.

"Why aren't you and Goofy working?" Mom asked.

"The trick contest is tomorrow," I said. "And he still hasn't learned anything." I sighed. "I think maybe Goofy is a dummy, Mom."

I whispered that last part so he wouldn't hear me.

"Roscoe, Goofy is the best dog in the

world," Mom said. "But he's just a dog. He can only do doggie things. If you work hard with him, maybe he can learn to fetch or shake hands. But mostly he's going to do what he does best—love you!"

"But he doesn't even know one letter, Mom!" I said.

Mom shook her head. "Maybe the problem isn't the student," she said. "Maybe the problem is the teacher."

"But I'm a good teacher!" I cried.

"That poodle you told me about—" Mom said.

"Edward."

"Edward," Mom said. "Edward wasn't reading, sweetie. It's just a trick his owner taught him. A good trick, but still a trick." Mom stood up. "I'm going to the garage to get some more mulch. I'll be right back."

I pictured that trophy. Shiny. Heavy. Gold.

If Goofy weren't so goofy, I could have that trophy.

Down the sidewalk I saw Martin and Edward. Martin waved.

He paused and said something to Edward.

Edward waved his little poodle paw at me.

Goofy ran over to say hello.

The old-fashioned dog way.

With major sniffing and tail wagging.

"Hey," I said. I gave Edward a pat.

Today he was wearing a pink-and-green sweater.

"Is that a white tiger on your sweater?" Martin asked.

"It's a panda," I said.

"It's like you've got a whole zoo on there," Martin said.

"Hey, how did you teach Edward to read?" I asked.

Martin just shrugged. "It's kind of a secret," he said.

"I'm trying to teach Goofy so he can be in the trick contest," I said. "But he's not a very good student."

Goofy licked my hand.

I felt awful for saying that about a friend.

"Don't get me wrong," I added. "He's the greatest. He just doesn't know his letters."

"Well," Martin said, "even Edward took a long time to learn."

"I wish I could take Edward to the contest," I said. "He'd for sure win."

Goofy sighed and lay down on the sidewalk.

I felt even worse.

Martin thought for a minute. Then he started grinning.

"You know," he said, "I might be able to let you borrow Edward."

I felt my eyes get wide. "You would let me borrow Edward for the contest?" I cried. "Name your price!"

Martin thought. "You know, I do like that sweater. It's very unusual."

I had to think for a minute. "You mean *this* sweater? This one I'm wearing? With smiley faces and monkeys on it?"

"Yep," said Martin. "It's one of a kind."

"That's for sure," I agreed. "But the thing is, my grandma knitted this for me. With love."

Martin shrugged. "That's okay. It was just an idea."

I pictured myself holding that shiny, glittering-in-the-sun, could-even-be-real-gold trophy.

I looked down at poor old goofy Goofy.

I checked over my shoulder.

Mom was back in the garden, busy mulching.

"No, wait," I whispered. "It's a deal. Follow me."

We went behind some tall bushes. Goofy and Edward came, too.

I took off my itchy, ugly sweater.

It was the best trade I'd ever made.

Except for the time I talked Hazel into giving me her double-scoop chocolate-chip-cookie-dough ice cream cone for a pink rubber band.

"Don't put it on till you get to the end of the street, okay?" I said.

Martin held up the sweater. "Is that a crocodile?" he asked.

"I think it's a rabbit," I said.

I touched the crocodile-rabbit's little nose.

"My tuba lesson is at ten tomorrow," Martin said. "I'll drop off Edward before I go."

"Great!" I said. "Ed, give me five!"

Edward put up his paw and we high-fived.

"It's Ed*ward*," Martin said. "Not Ed."

I'm not sure, but I think maybe Goofy groaned.

Goofy and I went back to the porch. I was cold.

On account of I didn't have my sweater anymore.

It was ugly and itchy. But it sure was warm.

"Roscoe," Mom said, "where's your sweater?"

"I—" I swallowed. "I, uh, took it off."

Which was true.

True-ish.

"It's chilly out here," Mom said. "You really need it."

"Goof and I are going in now, anyway," I said. "I think he's had enough learning. See you, Mom."

Goofy and I ran inside. I closed the door behind me.

In the hallway was a picture of me and Max and Hazel and my grandma and grandpa at a baseball game.

I thought about Grandma knitting all those furry little animals and smiley faces.

It probably took her a very long time.

She'd made that panda special. Because I was in the Panda reading group.

Martin would never even know that.

10

The Toe-Tapping Trick

It was warm and sunny on Saturday morning.

That was a good thing.

Because I didn't need to wear my sweater.

And because when Martin brought Edward over, Martin wasn't wearing my sweater.

His sweater, I mean.

"I'll pick Edward up after my tuba lesson," Martin said.

I took Edward's leash.

"Hey, did you know that sweater has 'I love you' written on the right sleeve in teensy yellow letters?" Martin asked.

"No," I said quietly.

"And I found a mouse and a raccoon on it," Martin said.

"That's not a mouse," I said. "It's a possum. My grandma and grandpa have a possum family living in their backyard."

"It's a great sweater," Martin said. "I wish Edward had one so we could match."

Today Edward was wearing a green T-shirt. It said "World's Smartest Dog" on it.

"Almost forgot," Martin said. He pulled

Frog on a Log out of his backpack.

"That's okay," I said. "I have a book he'll like even better. It's Goofy's favorite. *Bad Cat Goes to the Vet.*"

"Well, there's something I need to tell you," Martin said. He made a throat noise. "See, Edward can't exactly read."

"What do you mean?" I asked.

What about my trophy? I was thinking.

"It's a trick. I just signal him how many times to bark," Martin said. "I count the words on a page. Then I tap my foot. If it says, 'Jump, frog, jump!' then I tap my foot three times. And Edward barks three times."

"So it only looks like he's reading," I said. "Oh."

I was disappointed.

I sort of liked believing dogs could read.

Also I could see how I'd been a little hard on Goofy.

"You'd better stick with *Frog on a Log* since Edward is used to it. It's a cool trick," Martin said. "I'm sure you guys will win."

Martin patted Edward's poodle pom-pom. "Be sure he gets plenty of water," he said. "He likes springwater. Cold. But not too cold."

"Goofy likes toilet water," I said. "He's very open-minded."

"He's a nice dog," Martin said.

Goofy licked Edward. Then he licked Martin. Then he licked me.

"Yes," I said. "He really is."

. . .

Dad drove me and Edward to the contest.

I'd told him and Mom a teensy little fib about why I was taking Edward instead of Goofy.

I said Martin had to go to his tuba lesson. So he couldn't take Edward to the contest.

Which was true.

Then I said I was doing Martin a favor. Because he really wanted Edward in the show, so he asked me to help out.

That part was not so true.

Mom and Max and Hazel were coming to the show later. But I had to get there early to sign up.

"I'll say this for you, Edward," Dad said as we parked. "You sure smell better than Goofy."

"I think he's wearing doggie perfume, Dad," I said.

The contest was in a park by the street fair. Dogs and kids were everywhere.

We walked over to a long table covered with paper and pencils. Dad helped me fill out a form so I could enter the contest.

A lady gave me a number to pin to my shirt. It was 13.

"Thirteen is not very lucky," I said.

"Could be your lucky number today," the lady said. "What's your dog's name?"

I started to say, "He's not my dog."

But instead I just said, "Edward."

As we walked toward the big field, Dad said, "Goofy looked a little forlorn as we drove away."

"What's *forlorn*?" I asked.

"It's how you feel when you think your boy doesn't like you anymore."

"Goofy couldn't win a trophy, Dad," I said.

As soon as I said it, I felt bad. Even though it was the truth.

"He could win for biggest appetite," Dad joked.

He gave me a hug. Then he patted Edward.

"Good luck, guys," he said. "We'll meet you after the contest. I'm going to go save some seats so we have a good view. See ya, Ed."

"It's Edward," I said.

"Figures," said Dad.

11

Truly Terrific Tricks

The dogs and their kids lined up in a special area.

The crowd got bigger.

I saw Gus and Emma. They waved.

I saw Mom and Hazel and Max.

They waved too.

Then I saw somebody else.

Goofy.

He wagged his tail and pulled on the leash Max was holding.

He barked hello.

I felt like I was on a playdate with the wrong friend.

I mean a *hang-out*.

Three judges sat in chairs behind a table. They had paper and pens and serious faces.

"Contestant number one," said a man on a loudspeaker. "Mary Lou Oliver and her dog, Moe."

Mary Lou and Moe went to the center of the field.

Moe rolled over. Then he played dead.

Next came Nico and Spinner. Spinner danced on his hind legs.

Noodles caught a Frisbee in midair.

Linus played a toy piano with his nose.

He was extra good.

But nobody was as good as Edward.

On the judges' table I could see lots of colored ribbons.

And one beautiful trophy.

It was silver. Not gold.

And smallish. Not huge.

But still, it was going to look great on my dresser.

And be a cool show-and-tell.

When other kids brought their ribbons and certificates and awards, I would have something to show at last.

More dogs did tricks.

My favorite was Astro. He chewed up a kid's homework for his trick.

On purpose.

But even that amazing trick couldn't

beat Edward's.

At last they called us.

"Roscoe Riley and his dog, Edward," the loudspeaker man said.

We walked onto the field. I turned toward the judges.

"Edward, the amazing reading dog, will now read from this book," I said.

The crowd made a "wow" noise.

The judges leaned forward.

I brought the book over so they could see the first page of *Frog on a Log*.

Then I took it back to Edward. I put the book in front of him.

"Open the book, Edward," I said.

Edward opened the book with his nose.

Just like I knew he would.

"Now read to us!" I said.

The first words in the story were "Frog on a log."

I tapped my foot four times. Just a little, so that only Edward could see.

He barked four times.

Just like I knew he would.

"He's right!" one of the judges exclaimed.

The crowd cheered.

And I knew right then that trophy was mine.

. . .

While we waited for the judges to make their decision, I went over to the stands to say hello to my family and Gus and Emma.

"You rocked!" Gus exclaimed. "You for-sure are going to win!"

"Not bad," Dad said, "for a dog who wears perfume."

People crowded around me. Everyone wanted to pat Edward.

"How did you teach him to do that?" a man asked.

"How long have you owned him?" a lady asked.

"Why is he wearing a T-shirt?" a boy asked.

I tried to answer all the questions. But it felt a little funny.

On account of I had to pretend I knew the answers. Like I really was Edward's owner.

"Do you have any other pets?" a little girl asked.

At least I knew the answer to that one.

"I have a dog named Goofy," I said. "He's over there."

I pointed. Goofy was sitting by Max's

feet. He looked sort of left out.

Maybe even forlorn.

"Can Goofy do cool tricks, too?" the little girl asked.

"Well, not exactly," I said. "He's still learning. But he's a really great guy."

"Ladies and gentlemen!" the loudspeaker man said. "It is time for the awarding of prizes. If your name is called, please come to the judges' table to accept your award."

One of the judges stood up. She held a microphone in one hand and ribbons in the other.

"I just want to say that it was very difficult to determine a winner in this year's contest. What we especially love seeing is the wonderful bonds between dogs and their owners. A dog learns best when he is loved and praised. And it's clear that all these dogs are very much loved."

I looked down at Edward.

He was standing perfectly still.

I looked over at Goofy.

He was trying to catch a fly in his mouth.

"Third prize goes to Linus and Larry Dunn!" the judge announced.

Everyone clapped. Larry ran over with Linus to accept a yellow ribbon.

"Second prize goes to Astro and Penelope Watson," the judge said. "But don't you dare use that trick to get out of doing your homework!"

Finally, my moment arrived.

"And our first-prize trophy goes to the amazing team of Roscoe Riley and his dog, Edward!"

It was just like I'd imagined it.

Applause.

Cheering.

Even some barking.

We dashed over to the judges.

The trophy wasn't as heavy as I thought.
In fact, I think maybe it was plastic.
But it was a silver trophy, and it was
mine.

12

My Dog

I held the trophy high in the air. Edward and I ran across the field to my family.

There was lots of back patting.

And high-fiving.

And way-to-going.

I felt pretty amazing. I was definitely going to be the star of show-and-tell.

Something cold touched my hand.

I looked down, and there was Goofy.

He was nudging me with his nose.

He wagged his tail like he was happy for me.

He even touched noses with Edward.

Good old Goofy.

I gave him a hug.

"Will the contestants please return to the judges' table for photographs?" said the loudspeaker guy.

"Come on, Edward," I said. "They want to take our picture."

Edward and I walked back to the judges.

"Sit, Edward," I said. And of course Edward sat.

"Congratulations, Roscoe," the lady judge said. "You and Edward must have a very special relationship."

"Well, I—," I began. "He's a nice dog, yeah."

I looked back at my family.

Goofy was watching me. He wagged his tail. Just a little.

I held up the trophy. It glittered in the sun.

Just like I'd imagined.

Then I set the trophy down on the table.

"Edward's a nice dog," I said, "but he's not *my* dog."

"What do you mean, son?" another judge asked.

"That's my dog," I said. "Over there. I just borrowed Edward because I wanted a trophy, but he's not mine, he's Martin's, and I really want my sweater back too."

The judges just looked at me.

"What sweater, sweetheart?" asked the

lady judge finally. "I'm afraid you've lost us. And which dog is really your dog?"

I handed her Edward's leash. "I'll show you," I said.

"Goofy!" I called. "Goofy! Come here, boy!"

Goofy yanked free of Max. He dashed across the field like he was going after Hector.

He leaped into my arms.

We fell back.

We rolled and rolled and rolled and rolled.

It was great.

Goofy licked my nose.

The crowd went wild.

"This," I said, "is MY dog."

13

The World's
Best Backward
Somersault Team

They gave the trophy to the homework-eating dog instead.

But Goofy and I got a special white ribbon.

On the bottom, one of the judges wrote WORLD'S BEST BACKWARD SOMERSAULT TEAM.

When Martin came to pick up Edward, I told him the whole story.

I also told him I was really sorry, but I wanted my sweater back.

I told him I would pay him my allowance for as long as it took.

Martin said that was okay. Because even though he liked the sweater, it was awfully itchy.

14

Good-Bye from Time-Out

When I told my mom and dad about trading Grandma's sweater for Edward, they were not happy.

They were also not happy about the part where I fibbed about Martin wanting me to enter Edward in the contest. Although they were proud of me for telling them the truth eventually.

Also, for telling the judges the truth.

They said I was getting very mature.

So I asked, Does that mean no more time-outs?

Here I am. So I guess you can tell what their answer was.

It felt good to get Grandma's sweater back. In fact, I'm wearing it right now. I found a baby turtle and a worm on it while I've been sitting here.

It really is a work of art.

Too bad it's so itchy.

I don't even mind being in time-out so much today.

'Cause Goofy's here with me.

He got sent to time-out, too.

Something about eating the hot dogs we were going to have for dinner.

Good old Goofy.

This book is for Austin
from his friends
Katherine and Goofy

Contents

1

Welcome to Time-Out

Yep. It's me. Roscoe Riley.

Stuck in time-out again.

And speaking of stuck, have I got a story for you!

A very sticky story.

See, my class went on a field trip to an apple farm.

A field trip is when you go somewhere

more fun than even recess and lunch put together.

We went to an apple farm so we could learn about where our food comes from.

Besides the pizza delivery guy.

All the kids went. And our teacher.

And some moms and dads to make sure we didn't get rowdy or do trouble-making.

I didn't get rowdy.

Well, maybe just once or twice.

But I *did* get into a teeny, tiny, practically invisible bit of trouble.

Who knew there was a rule about not jumping into a giant tub of applesauce?

I'll bet you've done some applesauce swimming, haven't you?

No?

Well, trust me on this. You should stick

to swimming in real, live swimming pools.

Applesauce is very . . . well, appley.

But maybe I should start at the beginning.

The part before I got apple-slimed.

Something You Should Know
Before We Get Started

Worms are good for fishing and for scaring little sisters and sometimes dads.

But they do not make a very good snack.

I hear they taste sort of like mushy macaroni.

Something Else You Should Know

Before We Get Started

Everybody loves plain applesauce.

And cinnamon applesauce.

And even raspberry-flavored applesauce.

But boy-flavored applesauce?

Not so much.

4

Happy Apple Orchard

When I first heard about our field trip, I was pretty excited.

Almost as excited as my teacher, Ms. Diz.

She told us about the trip in a very thrilled way, with tons of exclamation points in her voice.

"Children!" Ms. Diz said first thing that morning. "I have a wonderful surprise! This

Friday we are going on a field trip! The first one for our class!" She grinned. "And the first one for me since I became a teacher!"

Ms. Diz is a brand-new teacher. I help her out whenever I can.

I know a lot because I am a retired kindergartner.

"My brother's class went on a trip to a bakery and they got free doughnuts," I said.

Then I raised my hand real quick because sometimes I forget to remember that part.

You aren't supposed to talk until you put your hand up in the air and wave it like crazy because that is better than just yelling at the top of your lungs.

"If we can't go on a bakery field trip, maybe a cotton-candy factory would be good. Or an aquarium with giant, kid-eating sharks," I added.

Sometimes my imagination button gets stuck on fast-forward.

"Those are great suggestions, Roscoe," said Ms. Diz. "But we've already made plans for this trip. I'll give you a hint, class. What have we been learning about the past few weeks?"

"If you squeeze your juice box hard, you get a gusher!" said Dewan.

"Do not pick your nose during snack time," Coco said.

For some reason, she looked right at me.

"The pencil sharpener is not for crayons," Gus offered.

Ms. Diz held up her hands to make a *T*. Like a coach taking a time-out.

She does that when she wants us to be

quiet. Which is pretty often, come to think of it.

"We've been learning about *where our food comes from*," Ms. Diz reminded us.

She said the last part very slowly. So our brains could catch up with her mouth.

"Remember we talked about how vegetables and fruits come from farms?" Ms. Diz asked. "And about how the farmers grow the food and pick it, then send it on trucks to stores where we can buy it? I know how much you guys love applesauce, and apple pies, and taffy apples," Ms. Diz said. "That's why we are going to visit—"

I finished for her. "THE GROCERY STORE!!!" I yelled. "I LOVE the grocery store because I push the cart for my mom and dad except not anymore because I knocked over a watermelon pile and that knocked over a lemon pile and whoa, that was cool because it looked just like pink lemonade!"

"Roscoe," said Ms. Diz while I stopped

to take a breath, "I need you to think before speaking. Okay?"

I thought for a while. "Okay!" I said after I figured I'd been thinking long enough.

"As I was trying to say," said Ms. Diz, "we are going to an apple orchard!"

"You mean where they make apples?" Gus asked.

"They don't *make* apples, they *grow* them," said Ms. Diz. "There are hundreds of apple trees at Happy Apple Orchard. They produce all kinds of apples. Green and red and yellow, sweet and sour. We'll each get to pick our own apples!"

That was way better than a field trip to a plain old field!

We did a lot of cheering and jumping out of our chairs and clapping.

Until Ms. Diz had to ring her gong.

It is a very loud bell that helps us Stay Focused.

Staying Focused is when you Stop Acting Like Preschoolers, Class.

"They make lots of food at Happy Apple too," Ms. Diz said when we were quiet. "We'll get to see them bake apple pies and make applesauce. We might even get to *eat* some! But only if you all are on your best behavior."

Pie and applesauce? That was too much great news.

Ms. Diz had to gong four times before we settled down.

But who could blame us?

We were going on a field trip to see happy apples!

5

The Magic Fortune-Telling Ball

When my brother, Max, and I got home from school that afternoon, my dad was in the kitchen.

Some days Dad works at home.

He says it makes him appreciate the office more.

"Dad!" I yelled. "We are going on a field

trip! My whole class!"

"Get a chocolate doughnut when you go," Max said. "The jelly ones are stale."

"We aren't going to a bakery," I said. "We are going to an apple maker."

"You mean an orchard?" Dad said. "Cool."

Max made a face. "Better luck next time."

"Sounds like fun to me," said Dad. "Roscoe will get to pick apples, I'll bet. And who knows? Maybe they'll have free taffy apples. Or free pie." He got a big smile on his face. "I do love a good apple pie. Especially a free one."

My little sister, Hazel, came into the kitchen. She was wearing a black pirate eye patch, overalls, a fluffy pink ballet tutu, and a pair of my dad's old sneakers.

"Hazel, my dear, as always you are looking very fashionable," Dad said.

If you ask me, little kids should not be
allowed to dress themselves.

"Did somebody say *pie*?" Hazel asked.

"I'm going on a field trip to an apple-
growing place," I explained. "They might
even give away pie and applesauce."

"Applesauce is my favorite," Hazel said.
"Except for gummi worms and broccoli."

Hazel pulled a small red ball out of one
of her pockets.

Hazel loved that ball. She carried it
everywhere she went. And she refused to
share it.

Of course, it wasn't just a plain old
everyday ball. It was a magic ball that
could tell the future.

All you had to do was shake it. Then

ask it a yes-or-no kind of question.

When you turned it over, there on the bottom, in a little bitty window, was your answer.

Hazel can't read yet. I think she just liked the ball because it was so shiny.

And because Max and I wanted to play with it.

"Magic ball, will I ever get to go on a field trip and eat pie?" Hazel asked.

She turned the ball over. "What does it say?" she asked Dad.

Dad looked at the bottom of the ball. "It says, 'YOU BETTER BELIEVE IT!'"

"Can I borrow your ball for one second?" I asked Hazel. "I just want to ask it about my field trip."

"Nope." Hazel shook her head.

"Please?" I begged. I smiled my best smile.

The one that makes Grandma say, "You old charmer, you!"

It works on grandmas.

But not so much on little sisters.

Hazel shook her head again. "Nope."

She tossed her ball in the air. When

she tried to catch it in her tutu, the ball dropped onto the floor.

It rolled behind the refrigerator.

"I'll get it for you, Hazel," Max said.

"No, wait! I'll get it!" I said quickly.

Because I am a helpful brother.

And also because I really wanted to get my hands on that ball.

"I have dibs," Max said.

"You just want it 'cause I want it," I said to Max.

"You just want it 'cause Hazel says you can't have it," Max replied.

It was hard to argue with that one.

"Besides," Max added, "you had a ball like that and you lost it."

"I didn't lose it," I said. "I accidentally dropped it in the garbage disposal when I was giving it a bath."

"We paid three hundred and twenty dollars to repair the disposal, if I recall correctly," said Dad.

"I don't want to get my tutu dirty," Hazel said. "Whoever gets the ball can play with it."

Max and I dashed to the refrigerator.

He took one side. I took the other.

We both reached for the ball.

I had to lie on the floor and s-t-r-e-t-c-h my left arm extra far.

When I stood up, I had dog hair, dust balls, and three Froot Loops stuck to my shirt. But I also had the ball.

I brushed off the hair and dust and ate the Froot Loops.

"Roscoe," Dad said, "please save the floor food for the dog. And why are you two so interested in that ball?"

"It's not just a ball, Dad," I said. "It's a ball that tells the future."

"I got it at Howie Hubble's birthday party," Hazel said. "'Cause I won pin-the-tail-on-the-donkey."

She started to take the ball from my hand.

"C'mon, Hazel," I begged. "You said whoever rescued the ball could play with it."

"You have got to promise, promise, PROMISE to give this back to me. Soon," Hazel said.

"How about Friday?" I asked.

"Promise?"

"I promise," I said. "You can count on me."

"Cross your heart and hope to fry?"

"Trust me, Hazel," I said.

"I trusted you with my Butterfly Barbie, and you let the dog eat one of her wings."

"That was a total accident. I wanted to see if she could fly," I explained. "And Goofy thought she was a Frisbee. I promise you that nothing will happen to this ball."

"Okay," she said, but she sounded like she didn't believe me.

I shook the magic ball. "Magic fortune-telling ball," I said, "will I have fun on my field trip?"

I turned the ball over and read the message.

"CONCENTRATE AND ASK AGAIN," it said.

I tried again. "Will I have fun at the apple orchard?"

"ABSOLUTELY, POSITIVELY YES!" it said.

Of course, I already knew that would be the answer.

6

One Hundred
Apples Up High
in a Tree

When our field-trip day finally came, I woke up extra early to be sure I wouldn't miss anything.

Turns out four in the morning is a little *too* early.

Moms and dads are very grumbly that time of day.

After I took the bus to school, we did the usual morning stuff.

The Pledge of a Wee Gent.

Morning Nouncements.

Calendar.

Weather.

And Sharing Time.

I shared Hazel's magic fortune-telling ball.

It was my second time sharing it.

But Ms. Diz said that was okay because I was clearly very attached to it.

Also, it was my last day of having the ball.

After school I had to give it back to Hazel.

She'd reminded me at breakfast.

Twice.

The first time I shared the ball, I had forgotten to ask it a yes-or-no question.

This time I asked it, "Will this be my

most funnest day ever?"

I turned it over and checked the answer. "'OUTLOOK CLOUDY,'" I read.

"It's going to rain?" Gus cried. "But that means no apple picking!"

"I think the ball means a different kind of cloudy," said Ms. Diz. "It means it's not sure what the answer is. But let's remember it's just a toy, and toys can't tell the

future. Besides, I think it's a pretty safe bet that today will be a fun day for all of you."

At last we lined up and headed outside to the field-trip bus.

I sat next to Emma. She's my best friend.

Gus sat in front of us. He's my other best friend.

Gus had to sit next to Wyatt.

Sometimes I call Wyatt "Bully Breath."

When I do that, Mom corrects me. "Let's just say that Wyatt does not exactly have a winning personality," she says.

But that's way too many words to remember.

Today we had to be polite to Wyatt because he was part of our apple-picking team.

On the bus there were some moms and dads, but my mom and dad couldn't come because they had to work.

Which was okay. Because sometimes parents can be embarrassing.

Like when they wipe your nose with a tissue when you have a perfectly good sleeve available.

Before we got going, Ms. Diz stood up at the front of the bus.

We were pretty exuberant.

Emma taught me that word. She likes words a lot.

It means "full of excitement."

Only *exuberant* sounds better.

We were so exuberant, I'll bet Ms. Diz wished she had her gong with her.

"I know you're all thrilled about our first field trip!" said Ms. Diz when we finally quieted down. "Now, when we first arrive at the orchard, we are going to listen to a lecture. After that we will pick apples. Do you all remember the rule we talked about?"

"Stay with your apple team!" we yelled.

"This is our very first field trip," Ms. Diz said. "So *please* let's be on our best behavior, okay, kids? No trouble, or we won't be able to have another trip someday."

The bus engine roared. We waved good-bye to our school.

"Happy apples, here we come!" I said.

All the way to the apple farm we sang a fun song.

It is called "One Hundred Apples Up High in a Tree."

Here is how it goes. In case you ever drive to an apple farm and need some entertainment.

One hundred apples up high in a
tree!
One hundred apples up high!
Take one down and pass it around.
Ninety-nine apples up high in a
tree!

Then you sing "Ninety-nine apples up high in a tree."

Then ninety-eight.

Then ninety-seven.

You keep on going until you get to "One apple up high in a tree."

And then—bam! You start all over again.

We sang that song a zillion times.

And nobody ever got tired of it.

Except I think maybe Coco's mom didn't like it so much.

On account of she put Kleenex in her ears.

7

Granny Smiths

Happy Apple Orchard had rows and rows of apple trees.

And a tour guy to show us how to pick apples. He had a green shirt with a red apple on the pocket.

His name was Abe.

Abe said apples are good for you. So it's not even cheating that they taste good too.

Abe showed us how the inside of the

apple has little black seeds in it.

Whole entire trees grow up from them!

Abe told us that the fuzzy part at the bottom of an apple is called a sepal.

He also said most of an apple is made of water, but there's some air in there too.

That's why apples float!

Finally the learning part was over and it was time to PICK!

Abe gave each team a big basket to carry their apples in.

"Now, here's what we're going to do," he said. "Each apple team will get their own tree. You may pick as many apples as you like, until your arms get tired or your basket is full. Whichever comes first."

Each of our apple teams had four people. And each team was named after a kind of apple.

There was a Golden Delicious Team.

And a Gala Team.

And a McIntosh Team.

We were the Granny Smith Team.

Granny Smith is the name of a sourish green apple.

It is probably the name of somebody's grandma too.

"These baskets hold a lot of apples, my friends. Do you think you will be able to pick that many?" Abe asked.

I pulled Hazel's magic fortune-telling ball out of my jeans pocket.

"Magic ball, will the Granny Smiths pick a whole basket of apples?" I asked.

I turned it over.

"It says 'NO WAY,'" I said.

"I'll bet you can do it," Abe said. "Especially with the help of a picking pole."

Abe passed each of us a long pole.

At the end of each pole was a little net.

Like a basketball net. Only closed up at the bottom.

"These are picking poles," said Abe. "Think of them as your apple catchers."

"And be very careful with them," Ms. Diz added.

"Now follow me, pickers!" Abe said.

He led us down a trail past lines of apple trees.

He stopped and pointed to a big tree. It had a zillion branches sticking out like big brown arms.

"Granny Smiths, you're first up," he said. "Meet your tree! These are called winesap apples."

It was cool and shadowy under the branches.

Red apples hung down everywhere.

Some were even on the ground.

"Don't eat the ones that have fallen," Abe warned. "They might be rotten. And don't eat the ones you pick from the trees until they've been washed."

Abe borrowed my picking pole and held it up high.

He tapped an apple. It plopped into the little net.

He lowered the stick and held up the apple.

"See?" he said. "That's how you do it. Easy as apple pie."

Abe looked more closely at the apple. "Oops. This one's a dud."

He tossed the apple over his shoulder. "There's a worm in that one. If you see an apple with a hole in it, there might be a worm inside."

The class made lots of *ewww!* noises.

"Okay, Granny Smiths," Abe said, "get to work. I'm going to take the other teams to their trees."

Let me tell you something. Those apples don't exactly *want* to get picked!

They must be pretty happy just hanging there like shiny decorations.

Because some of them hold on awfully tight.

After a while I figured out how to tap

hard with my apple picker.

An apple fell right in!

I pulled down my stick. There in my net was a bright red apple.

It even had a tiny green leaf on the stem.

I put it in our basket.

Emma and Gus and Wyatt each put an apple in too.

"My apple's bigger than your puny one," Wyatt said to me.

I decided to ignore him.

That's usually the best way to deal with Wyatt.

"We'll have a full basket in no time!" Emma said.

I gathered more apples.

One. Two. Three. Four.

It's a whole lot easier just to buy one of those bags of apples at the grocery store.

I was on apple number ten when I heard Wyatt yell, "Look at this sucker!"

He held a great big apple in front of my face.

It was awfully big, I had to admit.

But then I saw an even better apple.

Way up high.

The biggest, shiniest, most juiciest apple in Happy Apple Orchard!

8

The Amazing Apple

I took a swing at that humongous apple and missed by a mile.

Then Wyatt saw it too.

"It's the hugest apple on the planet!" Wyatt cried.

"It's *my* apple!" I said.

"Not if I'm the one who picks it!" he said.

We both swung our sticks at that

gigantic apple.

And we both missed.

We swung again.

Crack! Our sticks hit with a loud whack.

"Boys," Ms. Diz warned, "careful with the sticks!"

"It's just one apple, you know," Emma said. "There are hundreds of apples on this tree."

"It's a super apple!" I corrected.

"It's Gigantor, the Killer Apple from Outer Space!" Wyatt added.

"Wow," Gus said. "It looks like a basketball!"

I swung and missed again.

"Guys," Emma said, "our basket is only half full. Everybody else has a ton of apples."

"But they don't have the Awesome, Amazing Super Apple!" Wyatt said.

He swung again and missed.

I had an idea.

"Gus," I said. "Come here. It's time for a ladder."

"We don't have a ladder," Gus pointed out.

"I'll be the ladder," I said.

I got down on my hands and knees.

"Oh." Gus grinned. "I get it."

Gus climbed up on my back. He used his stick for balance.

"Ow," I said. "Ow, ow, ow. Hurry, Gus. Your ladder can't take much more of this."

Whack! Whack! Whack!

Gus kept missing. "Keep still. It's hard to balance when your ladder keeps breathing," he complained.

"Hey, it's cheating if you have to step on a friend," Wyatt said.

"I don't mind," I said.

Even though Gus was turning out to be way heavier than I'd expected.

"Emma," Wyatt said. "Come here. I need to step on you."

"Excuse me? Emma said. She laughed. "No way, Wyatt."

Wyatt turned to Gus.

"Gus," he said. "We need to work together. Stay on Roscoe. I'll climb on your shoulders and whack that apple down."

"How about I climb on you?" Gus asked.

"How about nobody else climbs on me?" I asked.

"I'm taller than you," Wyatt said to Gus.

Gus nodded. "Can't argue with that."

"Yes you can," said Emma. "And are you three aware that this is dumb?"

"I agree with Emma," I said with a groan. "And my back agrees too."

Just then somebody yelled a cover-your-ears kind of yell. "OUCH! I'm hit! Call 9-1-1!"

Emma went to find out what was going on.

"It's just Coco," Emma said when she came back. "An apple fell on her head."

Wyatt glanced over his shoulder.

301

All the teachers and parents were busy with Coco.

"The coast is clear," said Wyatt. "Stand still, Gus."

Gus stayed on me.

Wyatt climbed on him.

"UGH," I said.

One kid is heavy.

Two kids is *too* heavy.

"I am thinking this is a way not-good idea," I said.

I wobbled.

Gus wobbled.

Wyatt wobbled and whacked.

Whack! Whack!

Plop!

"I GOT IT!" Wyatt yelled.

Just before he fell.

And Gus fell.

On me.

"Ouch," I said.

"YOU ouch? What about ME?" Wyatt said, rubbing his elbow. "I was on top."

"Yeah, but I was on the bottom," I said with a groan.

Ms. Diz ran over.

"Boys, what on earth is going on here?" she asked.

"Check out this apple, Ms. Diz!" Wyatt cried.

He pulled that beauty out of the net.

"Let's eat it!" I said.

"Roscoe Riley!" Ms. Diz said. "The apples have to be washed first."

"It's bigger than a melon," Gus said.

"It's bigger than a Halloween pumpkin," I said.

"It's just an apple!" Emma said.

"No more misbehaving, boys," Ms. Diz warned.

"Sorry," we all said.

"You want to be able to go on other field trips, don't you?" Ms. Diz added.

"I vote for the doughnut place next time," I said.

"We'll see," said Ms. Diz. "It will depend on how much I can trust you to behave."

"Five more minutes of picking!" called Abe.

Which was good news.

My arms were tired. And so was my back.

Plus I was kind of sore from being smushed.

I guess Gus and Wyatt were tired too.

Because they sat on the ground with me while Emma kept picking.

I think maybe she's tougher than us guys.

Thanks to Emma, we got that basket almost filled.

But not quite.

"The magic fortune-telling ball was right!" I said. "We didn't fill our basket. But we did get the giant apple."

"Can I see that ball?" Emma asked.

I took it out of my pocket and handed it to her.

She shook the ball. "Magic ball," Emma said, "who should get to take home most of the apples since she did all the work?"

Emma turned over the ball. She grinned. "'EMMA SHOULD, BECAUSE THOSE GUYS WERE BUSY FIGHTING LIKE MORONS OVER AN APPLE,'" she read.

I am pretty sure she was just pretending, though.

Because that is for sure not a yes-or-no kind of answer.

9

Why You Should Never Eat an Apple with a Hole in It

Abe led us to a wide, long building.

An apple tree was painted on its front door.

Emma and Gus carried our almost-but-not-quite-full basket.

I carried our picking poles.

Wyatt carried the Amazing Apple.

The building smelled yummy inside.

Like cinnamon applesauce and taffy apples.

We set our baskets by the door. Abe gathered up our poles.

"This is where we clean our apples," he said. "We sort them here too. Some of the apples are too little to sell. We use those to make applesauce."

"Do we get to eat some free applesauce?" I asked.

"You sure do," said Abe. "We make applesauce in the room next to this one."

Abe waved for us to follow him. He paused in front of a big glass window.

On the other side we could see giant pots of gooey appley-looking stuff.

"That's the applesauce mixture after it's

been cooked. It's cooled off, and sugar and cinnamon have been added. Next it will go into containers to be sold," Abe explained.

He led us to a huge tub of bubbly water. It was as big as a wading pool. And as high as my belly button.

Apples floated in the water like little boats.

It looked like we were going to have a giant dunking-for-apples Halloween party.

Next to the tub was another one filled with plain water.

After that came a long moving belt.

It looked just like the conveyor belts at the grocery store checkout line.

This one was covered with apples, though, instead of milk cartons and dog food and toilet paper.

I felt in my pocket. The magic fortune-telling ball was still there, safe and sound.

So far, it had been right about whether this would be a good field trip.

I was *definitely* having fun.

"This tub is where the apples get washed," Abe explained. "Think of it as a big apple bathtub."

"Can I wash my Amazing Apple, Abe?"

Wyatt asked.

"*Our* Amazing Apple," I corrected.

Wyatt held up the apple so Abe could see it.

"Whoa, that *is* a big fella," said Abe.

Ms. Diz said, "Boys, every child will take home a bag of apples. Your moms and dads can wash them when you get home, and then you can eat them."

"Here's an idea," Abe said. "Why don't we run this big ol' apple through the wash? It's so huge, the kids might be able to keep track of it. Go ahead, young man. Throw it in the vat with all the bubbles."

Wyatt tossed the apple into the bubbly tub.

Plop!

It disappeared, then floated to the surface.

"Boys and girls," Abe said, "keep your eye on the apple. First it will be washed in this tub. Then it will move on to be rinsed."

The apple disappeared into a metal tube.

Abe led us to the second huge tub. This one didn't have any bubbles.

"There it is!" Gus cried. "I see it!"

Everyone cheered for the Amazing Apple as it bobbed in the water.

It looked extra shiny after its bath.

"Next it will go to the conveyor belt to be sorted," said Abe. "Follow me!"

The conveyor belt was loaded with wet apples.

Workers with white hats and coats stood by the belt.

They grabbed and tossed and grabbed and tossed.

"If they see a bad apple, they remove it,"

Abe explained.

That would be a tough job, I decided.

They all just looked like nice, happy apples to me.

"All these apples are making me hungry!" Coco said. "Can we eat soon, Ms. Diz?"

"We're almost done with our tour, Coco," said Ms. Diz.

Suddenly the Amazing Apple appeared on the conveyor belt.

"There it is again!" I yelled.

Abe pointed to the Amazing Apple and asked a worker to grab it.

The worker tossed it to Abe. Abe tossed it to Wyatt.

Wyatt looked at the apple. He didn't seem that thrilled about having it back.

"It's all yours," Abe said to Wyatt.

"Ready to eat."

Wyatt looked over at Coco. "Hey, Coco," he said, "you're so hungry. Why don't you eat it?"

It was nice, seeing Wyatt be nice.

Unusual too.

Wyatt tossed the apple to Coco.

"Thank you, Wyatt," she said.

She took a great big, mouth-open-as-wide-as-possible bite of that beautiful Amazing Apple.

She chewed.

And chewed.

"Good, huh?" said Abe. "Isn't that the best apple you ever tasted?"

Coco made a face. "It tastes like . . . macaroni!"

She looked at the apple and gasped.

"EWWWWWWWWW!" she screeched.

The apple dropped to the floor. "I ATE A WORM, MS. DIZ! I'M GOING TO DIE!"

"I think I'm going to faint," said Coco's mom.

If anybody had the right to faint, I figured it should be Coco.

"You'll be okay, young lady," Abe said. "It's just a little protein. Nothing to worry about."

"Wyatt," Ms. Diz said, "did you *know* that apple had a worm in it?"

"YOU POISONED ME!" Coco yelled at Wyatt.

"How could I know if it had a worm in it?" Wyatt asked.

He made an innocent don't-blame-me face.

I know that face. I've used it before.

Wyatt picked the apple up off the floor. "Besides, it's not like Coco ate the whole worm. Half of him's still in the apple."

"I don't feel so good," Coco moaned.

Everyone was looking at her. And you could tell they were all thinking, *I'M SO GLAD I'M NOT YOU RIGHT NOW.*

Even though Coco can be annoying sometimes, she didn't deserve to eat a worm.

Or even half a worm.

I pulled Hazel's magic ball out of my pocket.

"Magic ball," I said, "did Wyatt know there was a worm in that apple?"

I turned the ball over.

"'ABSOLUTELY, POSITIVELY YES!'" I read.

"Let me see that stupid ball!" Wyatt cried.

But before he could say anything else, someone fainted.

And it wasn't Coco's mom.

10

Boy-Flavored Applesauce

Coco lay on the floor.

"My baby's fainted!" Coco's mom cried.

Everyone crowded around to see what a fainted person looked like.

"Give her air!" Abe cried.

Wyatt looked at Coco. Then he looked at me.

"Let me see that ball," he repeated.

"No way!" I said. "It's my sister's."

Wyatt grabbed for the ball.

I turned and ran.

Nobody paid any attention. On account of Coco was busy fainting.

I zipped into the applesauce room to get away from Wyatt.

But he was right behind me.

A giant, loud machine was smushing apples.

Another one was stirring a huge tub of apple stuff.

It smelled sweet and cinnamony.

"Step away from the applesauce!" a loudspeaker voice yelled. "STEP AWAY FROM THE APPLESAUCE!"

I stopped running.

Wyatt tried to stop running too.

But he skidded on a slick spot.

Applesauce, probably.

He slid right into me.

Hazel's magic fortune-telling ball went flying.

Straight into the giant tub of applesauce.

It sank like a little red submarine.

"NO!" I screamed. "The magic ball!"

"STEP AWAY FROM THE APPLE-SAUCE!" the voice said again.

I couldn't jump in, could I?

Ms. Diz really wanted us to be on our best behavior.

I was pretty sure jumping into apple-sauce didn't count as best behavior.

On the other hand, I'd promised Hazel I would return her ball to her safe and sound.

Hazel was my little sister. She trusted me.

And she loved that ball.

There was only one thing I could do.

I leaped right into that giant tub.

The applesauce came up to my waist.

It was slimy. And oozy.

And tasty.

I reached down with both hands and felt the bottom.

But it was a very big tub.

And a very little ball.

I glared at Wyatt with mad eyes.

"You . . . you . . . you do NOT have a very winning personality!" I yelled.

I grabbed a handful of applesauce and flung it.

It landed—*splat!*—on Wyatt's face.

He scooped some off and tasted it.

"Not bad," he said.

"Bully breath," I muttered.

"Goo swimmer," he said.

"Ball stealer," I said.

"You have applesauce in your eyebrows," Wyatt said.

"You have applesauce in your nose hole," I said.

I smiled just a little.

So did he. Just a little.

"What's it like in there?" Wyatt asked.

"Gooey," I said.

"I can't believe you jumped in," Wyatt said in an admiring voice.

"Want some help?" he asked.

"Sure," I said.

Wyatt hopped in.

"WE HAVE A CODE RED IN THE APPLESAUCE ROOM! THERE ARE CHILDREN IN THE APPLESAUCE!" said the loudspeaker voice. "REPEAT: THERE ARE CHILDREN IN THE APPLESAUCE!"

We both looked for the ball.

I stuck my head all the way under the applesauce.

I couldn't see anything. But I could reach a little farther.

I felt something roundish and slippery-smooth.

There it was at last! The magic ball.

Safe and sound, but sticky.

When I came up for air, everyone was there.

Ms. Diz. The moms. The dads. Abe. The white-coated workers.

Even Coco.

Their mouths were open.

They stared and stared, but nobody said a word.

I guess we looked a little slimy.

"Do we still get our free applesauce?" I asked.

11

Good-Bye from Time-Out

So that's how I ended up going for my applesauce swim.

And landed here in time-out.

My hair was pretty sticky when I got home.

So was Hazel's magic fortune-telling ball.

I think maybe some applesauce got stuck inside of it.

Because now when you ask it a question, it only has one answer: "ASK AGAIN LATER."

Hazel was awfully nice about it, though.

When I said, "Can I borrow it again sometime?" Dad said, "Ask again later."

My whole family's visiting the orchard next weekend.

Wyatt and his family are coming too.

We are going to pick enough apples to pay for the applesauce we ruined when we swam in it.

Apparently, nobody wants Roscoe-and-Wyatt-flavored applesauce.

So they had to throw the whole batch out.

That means we have to pick seven whole baskets of apples.

Emma's coming with us to the orchard.

She says the only way we're going to get that many apples is with her help.

I think maybe she's right.

Ms. Diz says Emma is a good buddy.

I have to agree with her on that one.

She also said our class might go on another field trip someday.

But not for a long time.

I am crossing my fingers for a chocolate-candy factory.

Think of the oozy, gooey chocolate everywhere!

How could I possibly get into trouble at a place like that?

RoScoE's
Time-Out
Activities!

10 WAY COOL THINGS THAT SOMEBODY SHOULD INVENT

by Me, Roscoe Riley

1. Chocolate spaghetti

2. A water slide for my bathtub

3. Popcorn-flavored bubble gum

4. Invisible spray (for broccoli and other emergencies)

5. Trampoline floors at school

6. Robots that pick up
dirty socks

7. Remote controls with a
MUTE button for little sisters

8. Remote controls with a MUTE
button for big brothers

9. One-size-fits-all head bobbles

10. Super-Mega-Gonzo
Glue Remover

10 SECRETS ABOUT ME YOU PROBABLY DON'T KNOW

by Me, Roscoe Riley

1. I am afraid of ladybugs.

2. I like to put ketchup on my cereal.

3. I have a pair of lucky Spider-Man underpants.

4. I always throw up on merry-go-rounds.

5. When I grow up I am going to marry Ms. Diz if she is interested.

6. My paper airplanes *always* crash.

7. I have three night-lights.

8. I can wiggle my ears.

9. I enjoy flossing.

10. I am going to keep Hamilton until I am 101 years old.

10 BOOKS I THINK DOGS WOULD LIKE TO READ

by Me, Roscoe Riley

1. Tomcats in Time-Out:
A Picture Book

2. The Amazing True Story of
the Dog Who Ate an Entire
Ham and Nobody Even Noticed

3. Doorknobs: A How-To Manual

4. The No Good, Very Bad Bathtub

5. The Cat in the Vat

10 COMPETITIONS WITH MY BIG BROTHER I AM PRETTY SURE I COULD WIN

by Me, Roscoe Riley

1. Who can produce the loudest armpit fart?

2. Who is the fastest at tongue twisters?*

3. Who can get the biggest wad of bubble gum stuck in his hair when blowing bubbles?

4. Who can make the coolest ugly face?

5. Who can make the biggest cannonball splash at the pool?

*Just in case you want to try it, here's my favorite tongue twister (say this as fast as you can!):

Toy boat toy boat toy boat toy boat toy boat toy boat

6. Who can eat the most corndogs
at our Fourth of July picnic
(without throwing up)?

7. Who is the cutest smiler in the family?
(Grandma could judge this one because I am
almost positive I am her favorite.)

8. Who knows the best joke?*

9. Who can make the most original Lego
construction? (Last week I made a
three-headed frog on a bicycle, although
so far nobody has guessed what he is.)

10. Who is the best brother on
the planet? (Okay, okay . . . maybe this one
should be a tie.)

*Also, here's my most favorite joke:

Question: Why did the chicken
cross the playground?

Answer: To get to the other slide!

MORE RULES TO LIVE BY

by Me, Roscoe Riley

#16—Don't sharpen your crayons
in the pencil sharpener.

#43—Never do a cartwheel at the
grocery store.

#70—Don't do your secret
handshake with your friends when
your class is taking a test.

#58—Never sing opera while your
dad is driving the car.

#21—Don't steal your brother's
favorite joke.

#33—Never bake a mud pie.

#67—Don't bring bugs into your house, even if you just want to make a snack for them.

#95—Never run a race right after eating dinner.

#48—Never play hide-and-seek with your mom's purse.

#29—Don't run up the down escalator.

#18—Don't bowl on the school bus.

#76—Never take your fish for a walk.

#103—Don't try to make ketchup soup.

#34—Never hide a secret extra dessert in your laundry basket.

#57—Don't yell at your brother in the library, even if he's being extra annoying.

#42—Never paint with your mom's makeup.

#26—Don't try to wrestle your pillow.

#88—Never play Frisbee with your dad's old records.

#39—Don't fill your birdfeeder with candy.

#61—Never let your dog bury your sister's toys.

#15—Don't let your dog pull you on your bike.

#72—Never fall asleep on a trampoline.

#36—Don't trade your backpack for a sandwich.

#27—Never bring dirt in your room, even if you want to grow grass.

#84—Don't try to eat all the cookies in one sitting.

344

#55—Never tickle your dad when he's asleep.

#49—Don't leave your stuffed animals in the yard overnight.

#68—Never taste your mom's lotion, even if it smells like candy.

#91—Don't put raisins in your brother's bed.

#52—Never cut your dog's hair.

#75—Don't play tag with a bee.

#23—Never play baseball with
an apple.

#41—Don't lick paintings, even if
they're of food.

#19—Never chase a squirrel.

#82—Don't surprise thumb
wrestle your teacher.

#31—Never let your little sister
pick out your outfit.

#54—Don't practice playing the
drums when your family is asleep.

#97—Never sneak up on your dog.

#63—Don't jump on Grandma
when she's cooking.

#86—Never use gummy worms
as fishing bait.

CAN YOU SPOT THE DIFFERENCE?

If you want to stay out of trouble, you need to be able to tell when something's wrong. Try to find the seven things that have changed between these pictures.

353

359

369

371

DID YOU FIND
THEM ALL?

374

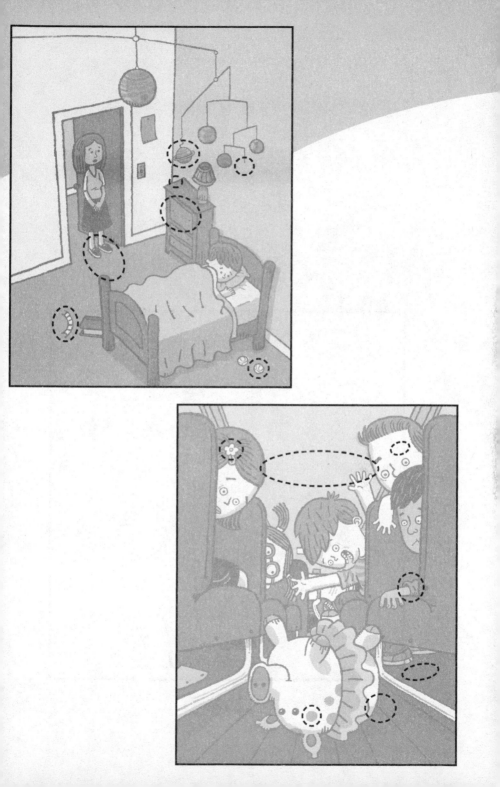

378

Stuck in time-out again! What went wrong this time?
Read all about my next adventure in

RoSCoE RiLEY
RULES

Don't Tap-Dance
on Your Teacher

1

Welcome to Time-Out

I can guess what you're thinking.

Time-out AGAIN? What rule did you break this time, Roscoe?

Well, since you asked, it was Rule Number 542: DO NOT PRETEND TO NEED CRUTCHES WHEN YOU REALLY DO NOT NEED THEM JUST TO GET OUT OF AN EMBARRASSING SITUATION.

Personally, I don't think a guy should get punished for breaking a rule when he didn't even exactly know there *was* such a rule.

But my mom and dad see things a little differently.

Sometimes I wonder if they ever really were kids.

You'd think people who used to be kids would understand that sometimes a guy just really needs a good crutch. Or two.

You know what I'm talking about, right?

Well, maybe it is a *little* confusing.

I'll begin at the beginning of the beginning.

With my friend Emma's amazing, noisy shoes . . .

2

Something You Should Know
Before We Get Started

Mom says girls can do anything boys can do.

Dad says boys can do anything girls can do.

Probably they're right.

Parents usually are.

But somebody needs to make sure kids

hear this news.

Kids need to know there's no such thing as just-for-boys stuff and just-for-girls stuff.

Like for instance, dancing elephants can be boys or girls.

Dancing mice too.

3

Something Else You Should Know
Before We Get Started

If you are pretending you smushed your leg, try to remember which leg is the limpy one and which one is not.

This advice may come in very handy someday.

4

Mr. Megaphone

The first time I heard Emma's tapping shoes was during show-and-tell.

Ms. Diz, my teacher, lets us bring all kinds of weird stuff to share with the class.

She is a brand-new teacher, so she likes to experiment on us.

Once Dewan brought a ferret. Which is

like a stretched-out guinea pig.

After that, Ms. Diz made up the No Show-and-Tells that Can Bite rule.

Maya brought her grandpa's artificial leg to another show-and-tell.

After that, Ms. Diz made up the No Show-and-Tells Without Permission of the Owner rule.

The same day Emma brought her new tap shoes to school, I brought something from my Noisy Stuff collection.

I always bring noisy stuff for show-and-tell.

I LOVE noise!

Weird noise.

Funny noise.

And of course, best of all, LOUD noise.

Here's what I've collected so far:

The newest addition to my Noisy Stuff collection is my Mr. Megaphone.

It looks like a giant ice-cream cone made of plastic.

When you talk into the mouth hole, it changes your voice so you sound like a megamonster.

A loud megamonster with a bad cold.

When it was my turn for show-and-tell, I yelled, "Take me to your leader, first graders of the Earth!" into the megaphone.

Half the class covered their ears.

The other half went "WHOA!"

"Roscoe, that's a fine addition to your Noisy Stuff collection," Ms. Diz said. "Thank you for sharing it."

"I can pass it around," I offered.

"Please, NO!" Ms. Diz said. "I mean, we have other people who want to share this morning. Speaking of things that make noise, Emma, you have something special to show us today, don't you?"

Emma held up two black shoes with metal tappers on the bottom.

"These are my tap shoes," she said. "They make noise when you step."

Shoes with built-in noise? I thought. *What will they think of next?*

And that's how it all began.

Stuck in time-out again! What went wrong this time?
Read all about my next adventure in

ROSCOE RILEY
RULES

#6

Never Walk in
Shoes That Talk

1
Welcome to Time-Out

You know, being stuck in time-out isn't so bad.

If you bring your imagination along for company.

Like right now.

I may *look* like I'm just sitting in my time-out corner.

But I'm pretending I'm playing baseball.

I just hit sixteen home runs in a row!

I am a baseball superstar.

I have a gazillion fans. I'm a very cool guy.

Inside my brain, anyway.

In real life, I'm a pretty ordinary guy, to tell the truth.

Although last week, I was one of the coolest kids in class for a while.

Actually, being cool is why I'm here in time-out.

Well, that's not exactly the reason.

I guess maybe the part where I destroyed my friend Gus's sneakers might have something to do with it.

I was just trying to help Gus be cool too.

You've smushed up shoes for a good reason before, haven't you?

No?

Not even to help out your best buddy?

I guess maybe this *does* sound a little strange.

Maybe I should back up a bit.

To when this all started.

The part before I was cool for two whole days.

Something You Should Know

Before We Get Started

When a TV ad tells you THESE SHOES WILL NEVER WEAR OUT, do not believe them.

When you have Destructo-feet, anything is possible.

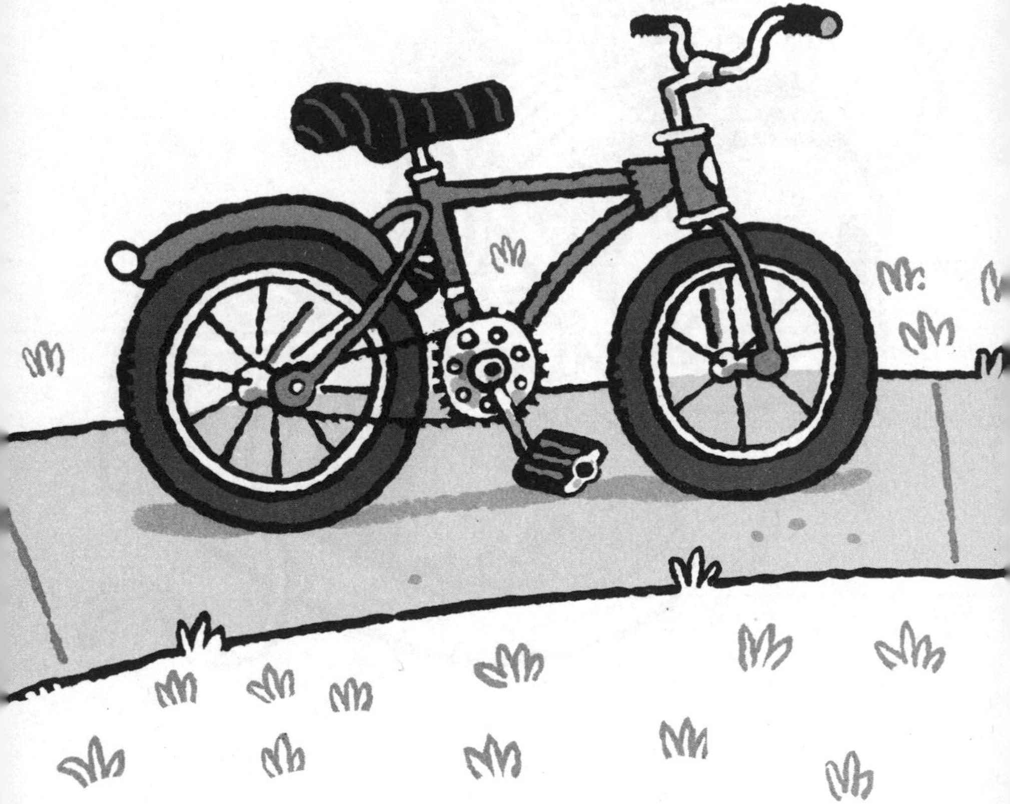

3

Something Else You Should Know
Before We Get Started

If you want to stop your bike, use your brakes.

Do not drag your toes on the ground to make it stop.

That is why brakes were invented.

That is all I have to say on the subject.

4

Uncool Shoes

Everything started one morning when I was putting my backpack in my cubby at school.

I heard Gus shout my name.

"Roscoe! You gotta see this! Hassan and Coco have talking shoes!"

Gus grabbed my arm and pulled. "Come on! This is major!"

Gus says lots of crazy things.

Once he told me he was pretty sure his guinea pig could count to ten in Spanish.

So when he told me two kids in our class had talking shoes, I wasn't all that surprised.

"They're called Walkie-Talkies," Gus said. "I saw them on TV. You will not believe the amazingness of these shoes!"

We ran into class.

And there before me was a whole new world of shoe possibilities.

Kids surrounded Hassan and Coco, who were each wearing a kind of sneaker I'd never seen before.

The shoes were made of shiny plastic. Like the boots my sister wears when it rains.

On one shoe was a big *W*.

On the other shoe was a big *T*.

There was a black push button near the toe of each shoe.

Coco's sneakers were pink. With glitter shoelaces.

Hassan's sneakers were blue with

lightning stripes.

Coco and Hassan were sitting in chairs on opposite sides of the room.

Coco had her left leg crossed over her knee.

She was whispering something into her shoe.

Which I have to admit looked pretty weird.

Hassan had his right leg crossed over his knee.

And here's the can-you-believe-it thing: Coco's voice was coming out of Hassan's shoe!

"See?" Gus whispered. "Walkie-Talkies! You talk into that little circle on the left shoe. It's sort of like talking into a cell phone. And if you have a friend with a pair of Walkie-Talkies on, they can hear you out of a little bitty speaker in their right toe!"

I did not even know what to say.

It was a science miracle.

Better even than Silly Putty.

Coco whispered something to her foot.

Hassan's shoe said, "I just *love* my Walkie-Talkies!"

Hassan's shoe.

Coco's voice.

Hassan grinned. "My dad got mine in Los Angeles on a business trip. Last time he just brought me a pack of peanuts and a cocktail napkin."

"Wow," I said.

"Yeah," Hassan agreed. "The only bad thing is that they are kind of uncomfortable. I have three blisters already."

"I have four," Coco said.

We sat there, oohing and aahing.

I knew what we were all thinking.

We were wondering what we could say to our parents that might make *them* say, "Hmm, this kid is so sweet I think I will run to the nearest store and buy him some Walkie-Talkies before they are all sold out."

I tried hard to think of something sweet to tell my dad.

He is getting balder every day.

Maybe I could tell him I'd noticed some fresh hair sprouts.

"My mom bought the last pair at Shoe Palace," Coco said. "They said they might get some more next week."

Ms. Diz, our teacher, came over to see what all the fuss was about.

"Why are you talking to your shoes?"

she asked in a polite way.

"This is the latest in fashion footwear, Ms. Diz!" said Coco.

"I can talk to Coco from anywhere in the room," Hassan said.

Ms. Diz frowned.

"Hmm. I'm not sure teachers are going to be too thrilled about this idea," she

said. "I liked the last shoe fad better. The ones that lit up. At least they were quiet!"

"What's a fad?" I asked.

"It's something that's very popular," Emma answered.

Emma knows all kinds of interesting words.

"Fads don't usually last very long," Ms. Diz added.

"I saw an ad for Walkie-Talkies on TV yesterday and asked my mom if I could get some," Gus said. "She said no. And then Babette spit up on Mom's bathrobe."

"How is your new baby sister doing, Gus?" Ms. Diz asked.

Gus shrugged. "It's just like when my little brother was born. Every time Babette burps, my parents think she's a genius."

"It's hard being a big brother," said Ms. Diz.

"It's hard being a little brother, too," I said. "We have to wear used-up big-brother clothes."

I looked down at my own boring shoes. Plain vanilla nothing-special sneakers.

They didn't even light up.

They were from the Ugliest Most Uncool Shoe Warehouse, I am pretty sure.

And my big brother, Max, had already worn them.

They weren't just preworn.

They were prestinked.

When you have to wear your big brother's yucky used clothes, it's called *hand-me-downs*.

Mom says it's also called *watching your spending*.

I am not sure what that means.

Except that it seems to involve making sure your kid will never be cool.

"Class, if we could all stop staring at Hassan's and Coco's feet for a while, we have spelling work to get started on," said Ms. Diz.

"We read you loud and clear, Ms. Diz," said Hassan's right foot.

Everybody laughed.

I would have given anything to have his blisters right about then.

Stuck in time-out again! What went wrong this time?
Read all about my next adventure in

ROSCOE RILEY
RULES

 #7   Never Race a
Runaway Pumpkin

1

Welcome to Time-Out

Hey, friend! Over here, in the time-out corner.

It's me, Roscoe.

I'm pretty sure I only have to stay in time-out for about three more minutes.

That should be plenty of time for me to tell you how I ended up here.

Oops.

Mom checked the clock. Turns out I have *seven* more minutes.

I thought seven was supposed to be a lucky number!

My teacher says when you think a number is lucky, that's called a *superstition*.

She says there's no such thing as a lucky number.

And that seven is just like eight and forty-seven and a gazillion.

A plain, old, everyday number.

I used to think lots of things were lucky.

Things like numbers and four-leaf clovers and horseshoes.

I used to think lots of things were *un-lucky*, too.

That's sort of how I ended up in time-out.

One thing led to another, and before

I knew it, I was being chased down the street by a humongous pumpkin.

And let me tell you, those guys can MOVE.

You've been chased by a giant piece of food before, haven't you?

No?

How about normal-size food?

Not even a little bitty grape?

Oh.

I guess being chased by food doesn't come up all that often.

But I can explain everything.

Have you got seven minutes to spare?

Something You Should Know
Before We Get Started

When a kitty rubs her face on your leg, she is just saying hello.

It does not mean she is wondering how you will taste for dinner.

3

Something Else You Should Know
Before We Get Started

A pumpkin is a fruit. Not a vegetable.

It's a true fact. I learned it at school.

But take it from me. When the biggest pumpkin in town is about to smush you into a pumpkin-boy pie, you don't really care if it's a fruit or a vegetable.

You just want to get out of its way.

4

Buzillions, Katrillions, and Other Cool Numbers

Sometimes I wish I hadn't gone to the school library last week.

Then I never would have seen the giant pumpkin that got me into so much trouble.

Don't get me wrong. I *love* our school library.

It's the most fun place in my school.

424

Except maybe for the playground.

Our library has maps. And DVDs. And CDs. And computers.

But most of all, it has tons of books.

My class goes there twice a week for story time.

Our story-time area is shaped like a little pirate ship. On the deck are lots of squishy pillows.

Mr. Page is the library helper who reads to us.

He has the best name for a library guy, I think.

Although *Mr. Shhh* would be good too.

When Mr. Page reads, he wears a black eye patch like a real pirate.

Also, he says, "ARGHH, me hearties!"

Which is Pirate for *Hello, kids!*

This time Mr. Page was wearing an

orange eye patch, though.

On account of the book he was going to read to us was about pumpkins.

"Okay, folks," said Mr. Page. "Today's book is called *Pumpkin Power*. It's full of fun facts about pumpkins."

He held up the book. The cover had a picture of a giant pumpkin on it.

"Before we start reading," said Mr. Page, "I want to tell you about an even bigger pumpkin!"

He unrolled a poster.

There was a photo of a boy and a girl on it.

They were each holding a book. And smiling.

And next to them was the most gigantic pumpkin I had ever seen. It looked huge!

It was as tall as my dad.

Almost.

And as big as our car.

Almost.

"That's got to be the world's biggest pumpkin," I cried.

"Actually, giant pumpkins can reach over one thousand six hundred pounds," said Mr. Page. "This one is gigantic, all right. But it's not *that* big."

"Any kind of gigantic is good, if you ask me," I said.

"This poster is from Hilltop Bookstore," Mr. Page said. "They're having a contest. If you guess the weight of the giant pumpkin in their window, you win books for the school library. Enough to fill that giant pumpkin!"

"That's a lot of books!" said Emma.

"You're right, Emma. And we sure could

use them," said Mr. Page. "You can make a guess when you visit the bookstore. The winner will be announced at the Fall Festival on Saturday."

"I'll bet that pumpkin weighs two hundred buzillion pounds!" Hassan said.

"Nunh-uh," said Gus. "Seven thousand katrillion pounds, at least."

Emma said, "I'm not sure if buzillion and katrillion are for-real numbers. But googol is a real number, right, Ms. Diz?"

Ms. Diz is our first-grade teacher.

She knows lots of math and spelling.

And also how to wiggle her ears.

"Googol *is* a number, Emma," Ms. Diz said. "A very big number. It has one hundred zeros in it!"

"That pumpkin is for sure a googol pounds then," I said.

"Children," said Ms. Diz, "maybe we should work on estimating how much things weigh. It could be a wonderful learning opportunity."

When Ms. Diz says *learning opportunity*, she gets very excited.

She is a brand-new teacher, so she likes to try out new ideas on us. Mostly that is a good thing.

But once she let us make marshmallow crispies so we could learn about measuring.

After that Learning Opportunity, she had to send home a letter to all the parents about How to Wash Marshmallow Goo out of Your Child's Hair.

"Kids, I forgot to mention that the contest winner also gets a prize," added Mr. Page. "Candy. Lots of it. Enough to fill the pumpkin."

"A googol pounds of candy!" said Gus.

He had a goofy smile on his face.

I probably did too.

"ARGHH, me hearties!" said Mr. Page in his pirate voice. "It's time to read!"

He held up the book so we could see the first page.

"'You may think that a pumpkin is a vegetable,'" he read. "'But it's really a fruit, because it has seeds inside of it.'"

Hmm, I thought. It was a very interesting fact.

But not nearly as interesting as the news about the contest.

Mr. Page kept on reading about pumpkins. He talked about giant pumpkins, tiny pumpkins, pumpkin seeds, and pumpkin pie.

My ears tried to pay attention.

But my brain kept thinking how nice it would be to win books for the library.

And candy for me.

Turn the page for a super-special look at
The One and Only Ivan, winner of the Newbery Medal
and a #1 *New York Times* bestseller!

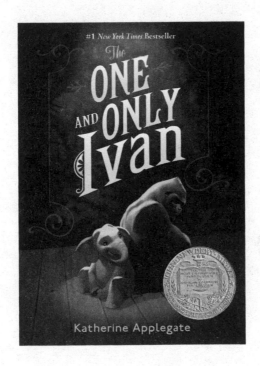

hello

I am Ivan. I am a gorilla.

It's not as easy as it looks.

names

People call me the Freeway Gorilla. The Ape at Exit 8. The One and Only Ivan, Mighty Silverback.

The names are mine, but they're not me. I am Ivan, just Ivan, only Ivan.

Humans waste words. They toss them like banana peels and leave them to rot.

Everyone knows the peels are the best part.

I suppose you think gorillas can't understand you. Of course, you also probably think we can't walk upright.

Try knuckle walking for an hour. You tell me: Which way is more fun?

patience

I've learned to understand human words over the
years, but understanding human speech is not the
same as understanding humans.

Humans speak too much. They chatter like
chimps, crowding the world with their noise even
when they have nothing to say.

It took me some time to recognize all those
human sounds, to weave words into things. But I
was patient.

Patient is a useful way to be when you're an ape.

Gorillas are as patient as stones. Humans, not so
much.

how I look

I used to be a wild gorilla, and I still look the part.

I have a gorilla's shy gaze, a gorilla's sly smile. I wear a snowy saddle of fur, the uniform of a silverback. When the sun warms my back, I cast a gorilla's majestic shadow.

In my size humans see a test of themselves. They hear fighting words on the wind, when all I'm thinking is how the late-day sun reminds me of a ripe nectarine.

I'm mightier than any human, four hundred pounds of pure power. My body looks made for battle. My arms, outstretched, span taller than the tallest human.

My family tree spreads wide as well. I am a great ape, and you are a great ape, and so are chimpanzees and orangutans and bonobos, all of us distant and distrustful cousins.

I know this is troubling.

I too find it hard to believe there is a connection across time and space, linking me to a race of ill-mannered clowns.

Chimps. There's no excuse for them.

KATHERINE APPLEGATE is the author of lots of books for kids, including the Roscoe Riley Rules series and *The One and Only Ivan*, which was awarded the 2013 Newbery Medal. Katherine lives in Northern California with her two terrific kids, one wacky dog, two cranky cats, and one patient husband. She has not been in time-out in quite a while, but her dog, Stan, was recently sent there for breaking rule #132: Never eat a Hula-Hoop. You can visit her online at www.katherineapplegate.com.

BRIAN BIGGS has illustrated more than fifty books written by many amazing authors and has written a few books himself. Growing up in Arkansas and Texas, Brian tried really hard to stay out of trouble. He did what his teachers and parents asked, he followed the rules, and he got good grades. Now he lives in Philadelphia with his wife and teenagers, where he spends his days drawing and writing in an old garage where he can pretty much do whatever he wants. You can visit him online at www.mrbiggs.com.

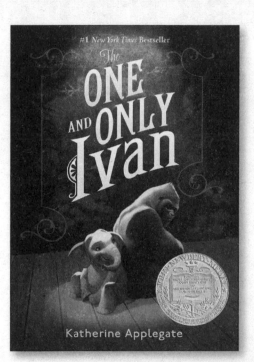

Roscoe Riley doesn't <u>mean</u> to break the rules.

Roscoe has a brand-new look!
Now with Roscoe's Time-Out Activities,
featuring bonus games, lists, and more!